Art by: Natasha Thornton, Age 12,
Southwood MS, Miami, FL
THE SCHOLASTIC ART & WRITING AWARDS
A Gift For MS. Singer
From Melanie.S. Year 05
SCHOLASTIC

Each Little Bird That Sings

Other Books by Deborah Wiles

One Wide Sky: A Bedtime Lullaby

Love, Ruby Lavender

Freedom Summer

Each Little Bird That Sings

DEBORAH WILES

Gulliver Books
Harcourt, Inc.
ORLANDO AUSTIN NEW YORK
SAN DIEGO TORONTO LONDON

www.HarcourtBooks.com

Gulliver Books is a trademark of Harcourt, Inc., registered in the United States of America and/or other jurisdictions.

Library of Congress Cataloging-in-Publication Data
Wiles, Debbie.
Each little bird that sings/Deborah Wiles.
p. cm.
"Gulliver Books."
Summary: Comfort Snowberger is well acquainted with death since her family runs the funeral parlor in their small southern town, but even so the ten-year-old is unprepared for the series of heart-wrenching events that begins on the first day of Easter vacation with the sudden death of her beloved great-uncle Edisto.
[1. Funeral homes—Fiction. 2. Death—Fiction. 3. Grief—Fiction. 4. Family life—Southern States—Fiction. 5. Southern States—Fiction.] I. Title.
PZ7.W6474Eac 2005
[Fic]—dc22 2004013631
ISBN 0-15-205113-9

Map drawn by Comfort Snowberger
with assistance from Peach Shuggars

Text set in Bembo
Designed by Lydia D'moch

C E G H F D

Printed in the United States of America

For

Liz Van Doren,

who stood vigil

through the dark wordless night

and

for Jim Pearce,

who sang to me

in the morning

ACKNOWLEDGMENTS

In the four years since the publication of *Love, Ruby Lavender,* one death followed another in my family and I came to understand the meaning of friendship and the power of love. I was suffocating in grief, unable to finish a story I had been trying to write for years—unable to finish anything. Friends and family slipped their arms around me, grabbed hands, and created a cradle from which I would eventually learn to navigate the world again and to write Comfort's story.

Sue Fortin came first. Four Lions met her at the door: Nancy Werlin, Jo Stanbridge, Dian Regan, and Janie Kurtz. Norma Chapman, Jackie Erskine, Deborah Hopkinson, the High-Test Girls, Norma Mazer,

Mike McConnell, Susan Miller, Judy Pontius, Linda Reed, Karen Robbins, and "The Voice" were witnesses to an ending that became a beginning. Together they created a lifeline for me. Cindy Powell pulled me to my feet. Kay Sheiss fed me and dispensed fashion advice. Kay and Cindy told the most raucous funeral stories I'd ever heard. Kay supplied the best first line ever for a novel. Plus, she has a snazzy maiden name. I borrowed it for Comfort's last name.

Lavonne Radonovich championed me in schools, as did teachers and librarians around the country. What good work we did together! Thousands of children wrote their stories of wonder, courage, and resilience. They taught me how to pay attention. My cousin Carol Booth (the pretty cousin) and friends at the Brandon, Mississippi, library claimed me as their own. I owe each of them an RC Cola and a packet of Tom's peanuts. Moon Pies and heartfelt thanks to everyone at Thurber House, Vermont College, and PEN, for the validation and support.

My family gave me hours, days, weeks, and finally months of time that belonged to them so I could finish this story. My daughter Hannah read the manuscript in its early drafts and gave her usual insightful comments. Friends and fellow writers Emily Ruppel and Iris Anne Debamie did the same.

My editor, "Dismay" Van Doren, was patient, steadfast, and definitely long-suffering. Every time I swooned, she flapped at my face with a Snowberger's handkerchief. Then she led me back to my chair clutching all the right questions to answer. She is an Editor-Dog Extraordinaire, bright and beautiful.

Jim Pearce, wise and wonderful, climbed a mountain with me and with this story and shouted a rallying cry every time I faded. He understood the silence. He laughed with me, praised my biscuits, read the entire first draft, and asked the most pivotal question: *Is there a dog?*

Without all these folks and those readers of *Love, Ruby Lavender* who wrote such loving letters to me, this book would not exist. As I emerged from that cradle and unfolded myself into the sweetness of new beginnings and the fullness that follows a fallow time, I began to understand, truly, how *family is a circle of friends who love you.* So here is a hymn to family: to kin well-known and kin yet to come. Thank you for opening your hearts to me, to my family, and to the power of story.

Each Little Bird That Sings

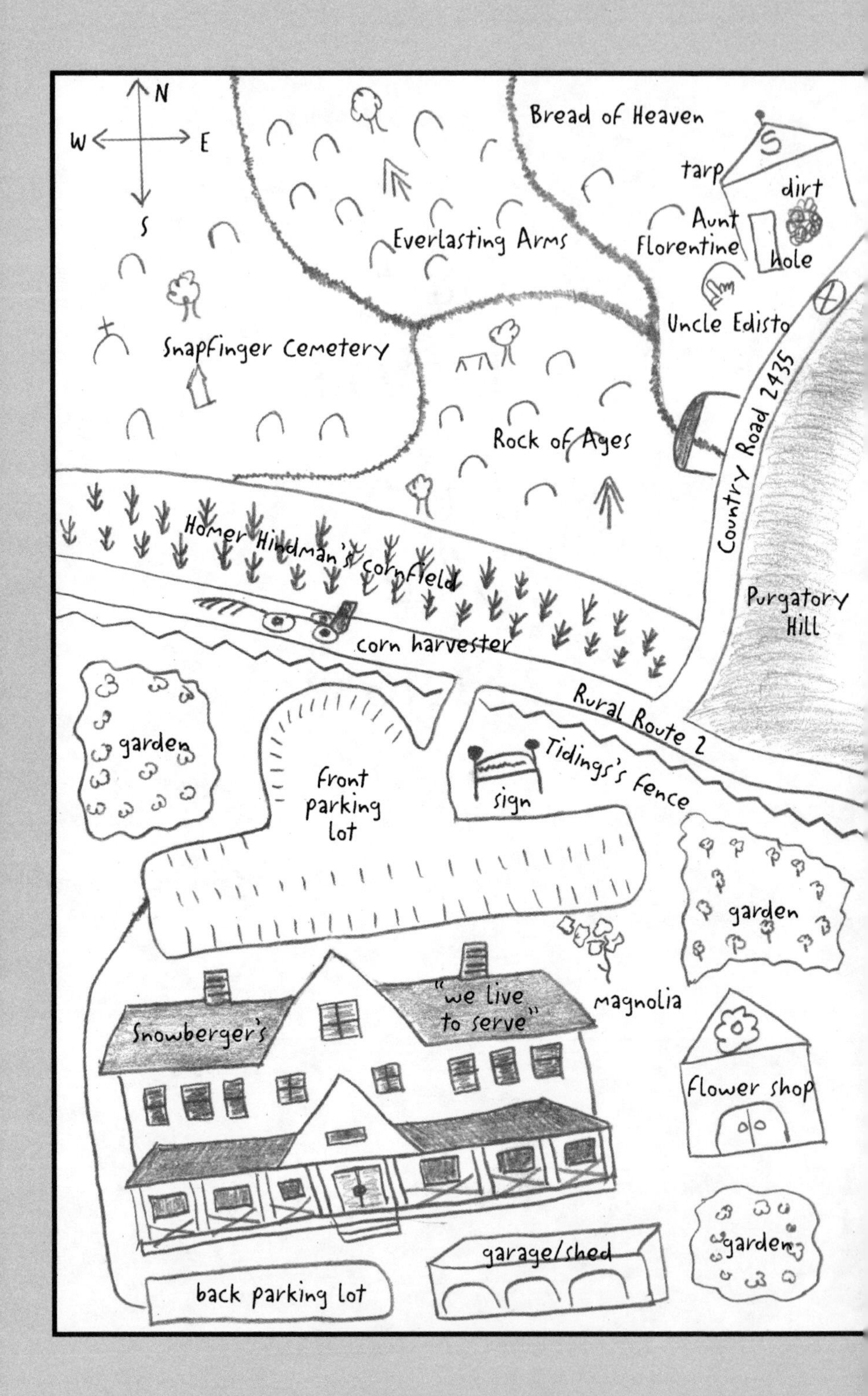
N
W
E
S
Bread of Heaven
tarp
S
dirt
Aunt Florentine
hole
Everlasting Arms
Uncle Edisto
Snapfinger Cemetery
Rock of Ages
Country Road 2435
Homer Hindman's cornfield
Purgatory Hill
corn harvester
Rural Route 2
Tidings's fence
garden
front parking lot
sign
garden
magnolia
"we live to serve"
Snowberger's
flower shop
garage/shed
garden
back parking lot

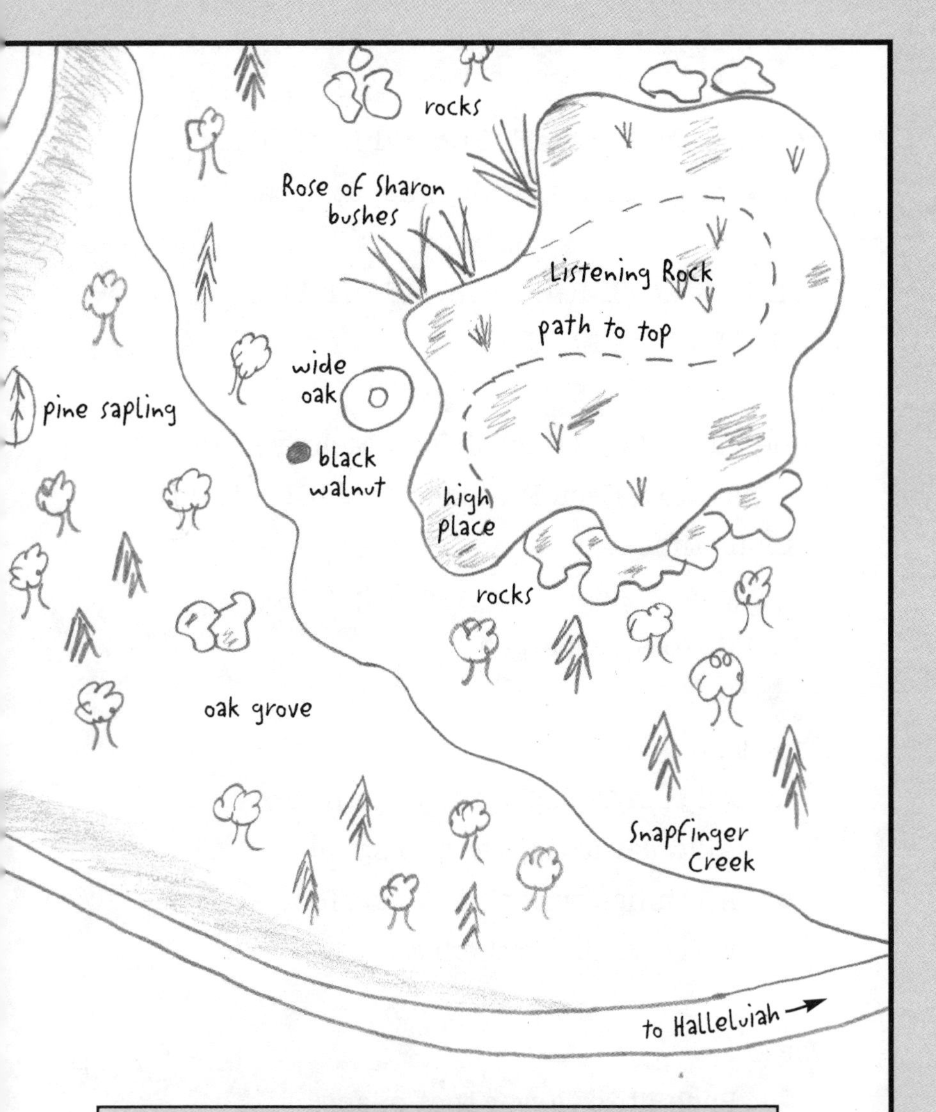

SNOWBERGER'S FUNERAL HOME EMPIRE,
Snapfinger, Mississippi

⊗ = argument spot

= hundreds of tombstones

= hundreds of oaks, sycamores, maples

= cemetery entrance

= hundreds of pines

Legend: not to scale

Song #72
from the Snowberger's Funeral Home Book
of Suggested Songs for Significant Occasions

ALL THINGS BRIGHT AND BEAUTIFUL
(AND TERRIBLE!)

Tune: Royal Oak (English Folk Melody)
Original Text: Cecil F. Alexander (1818–1895),
a long time ago
Slightly Revised and Lovingly Updated
by Edisto Snowberger

Chorus:

All things bright and beautiful,
All creatures great and small,
All things wise and wonderful:
We're family to them all!

Verse 1:

Each little flower that opens,
Each little bird that sings,
How resplendent are their colors!
How magnificent their wings!

(Chorus)

Verse 2:

The purple-headed mountains,
The river rushing by,
The sunset, and the morning,
That brightens up the sky!

(Chorus)

Verse 3:

The biting wind in winter,
The scorching summer sun,
The ripe fruits in the garden:
They're cousins! Every one!

(Chorus)

Verse 4:

The thorny bushes that snag us,
The knees we skin when we play,
The snakes that hiss, the kin we kiss,
All lovable in their way!

(Chorus)

CHAPTER 1

I come from a family with a lot of dead people.

Great-uncle Edisto keeled over with a stroke on a Saturday morning after breakfast last March. Six months later, Great-great-aunt Florentine died—just like that—in the vegetable garden. And, of course, there are all the dead people who rest temporarily downstairs, until they go off to the Snapfinger Cemetery. I'm related to them, too. Uncle Edisto always told me, "Everybody's kin, Comfort."

Downstairs at Snowberger's, my daddy deals with death by misadventure, illness, and natural causes galore. Sometimes I ask him how somebody died. He tells me, then he says, "It's not how you die that makes the important impression, Comfort; it's how you *live.* Now go live awhile, honey, and let me get back to work." But I'm getting ahead of myself. Let me back up. I'll start with Great-uncle Edisto and last March, since that death involves me—I witnessed it.

It was March 27, the first day of Easter vacation. I had just finished deviling eggs in the upstairs kitchen. Uncle Edisto and I were planning the first picnic of spring. My best friend, Declaration Johnson, would be joining us. I was sitting at the kitchen table, scarfing down my Chocolate Buzz Krispies. Uncle Edisto licked the end of his pencil and scribbled onto the crossword puzzle in the *Aurora County News.* Daddy and Mama were working. Great-great-aunt Florentine had just sneaked her ritual piece of bacon from the paper-toweled rack by the stove.

"I'm off to the garden, darlin's!" she said. "I feel a need to sing to the peas!" She kissed Great-uncle Edisto's head. He looked up from his crossword puzzle and sang—to the tune of "Oh! Susanna"—"Oh, Peas-Anna! Don't you cry for me . . ." I laughed with my mouth full of cereal. Aunt Florentine blew me a kiss, then she drifted out of the room, singing to herself: "For I come from Mississippi with a Moon Pie on my knee!"

"'Moon Pie'!" said Uncle Edisto, poising his pencil over the crossword puzzle. "That's it! Twenty-four across!"

The sky had been clouding up all morning, but I was ignoring all signs of rain. A grumble of thunder brought my dog, Dismay, to the kitchen, where he shoved himself at my feet under the table, pressed his shaggy black body against my legs, and shuddered.

"Oh, now, doggie!" said Great-uncle Edisto, peering under the table at Dismay. "You don't have to worry about no thunder! It's a beautiful day for a pic-a-nic!" Uncle Edisto was always optimistic. "Yessir," he said, smiling at me, "a pic-a-nic at Listening Rock should be just about perfect today!"

Then—*Craaaack!* went the thunder. *Sizzle!* went the lightning. And *Boom!* . . . The sky opened wide and rain sheared down like curtains.

Dismay scrambled for my lap, bobbling the kitchen table on his back.

"Whoa, doggie!" called Great-uncle Edisto. He steadied the table as Dismay yelped and tried to get out from *under* the table and *onto* me.

"Down, Dismay!" I shouted. Milk sloshed out of my bowl, and I made a mighty *push-back* in my chair. Dismay's toenails clawed my legs and his thick coat crammed itself into my nose as my chair tipped sideways with me and Dismay in it. *"Umpgh!"* The air left my body. My Snowberger's baseball cap popped right off my head. And there I was, lying on the kitchen floor with a sixty-five-pound dog in my face. He stuck his shaggy snout into my neck and shivered. An obituary headline flashed into my mind: *Local Girl, 10, Done In by Storm and Petrified Pet!*

Into the middle of all this commotion clomped my little sister, Merry, wearing Mama's high heels and a red slip that pooled around her feet. I peeked at her from under my dog blanket. As soon as she saw me, her eyebrows popped high and her mouth rounded into a tiny O of surprise.

"Dead!" she said.

"No," I said. I spit out dog hair. It was fine and silky and tasted like the cow pond.

"You all right, Comfort?" Great-uncle Edisto towered over me. He wore fat blue suspenders, and I could smell his old-person-after-shaving smell.

"I'm okay."

My head hurt. My plans were ruined. My dog was overwrought. But other than that, I was fine.

"Fumfort!" chirped Merry.

"Move, Dismay!" I pushed at him, but Dismay was

glued to me like Elmer's. He gave my face three quick licks with his wet tongue, as if to say, *Yep, it's thunder! Yep, it's thunder!! Yep, it's thunder!!!*

Merry turned herself around and stomped out of the kitchen, singing, to the tune of "Jingle Bells": "Fumfort dead, Fumfort dead, Fumfort dead away!"

Downstairs the front doors slammed, and my older brother, Tidings, who had been painting the fence by the front parking lot, yelled, "Attention, all personnel! Where are the *big* umbrellas! I need rain cover!"

Dismay immediately detached himself from me and scuttled for the grand front staircase to find Tidings, who was bigger than I was and who offered more protection.

I gazed at the ceiling and took stock of the situation. One: It was raining hard. There went my picnic. Two: Best friend or not, Declaration would not come over in the rain—she didn't like to get wet. There went my plans. Three: I didn't have a three, but if I thought about it long enough, I would.

Great-uncle Edisto extended a knobby hand to me and winced as he pulled me to my feet. He gave me my baseball cap, and I used both hands to pull it back onto my head.

"You're gettin' to be a big girl," he said. He picked

up the newspaper, tucked his pencil behind his ear, and looked out at the downpour. His voice took on a thoughtful tone. "The rain serves us."

Great-uncle Edisto always talked like that. Everything, even death, served us, according to him. Everything had a grand purpose, and there was nothing amiss in the universe; it was our job to adjust to whatever came our way. I didn't get it.

"We can have us some deviled eggs and tuner-fish sandwiches right here in the kitchen, Comfort," he went on. "Or, we can try another day for that pic-a-nic."

When I didn't answer, he turned his head to find me. "What's the matter, honey?"

"I'm disappointed." I studied my scratched-up legs.

"So am I!" Great-uncle Edisto took a Snowberger's handkerchief out of his shirt pocket and mopped at his face. "I like to pic-a-nic more than a bee likes to bumble!"

He did.

While we straightened the table and chairs and cleaned up the spilled cereal, Great-uncle Edisto told me about how disappointments can be good things—like the time he thought he'd planted Abraham Lincoln tomato plants in the garden but found out later they were really Sunsweet cherry tomatoes. He'd had his heart set on sinking his teeth into those fat Abe Lincoln tomatoes, but then he discovered that he liked the Sunsweets even better—and besides, he could pop a whole Sunsweet into his mouth at once and save his front teeth some wear and tear. "A distinct advantage at my age," he said.

"That doesn't help my mood," I said. The rain pounded so hard on the tin roof, it made a roaring sound inside the kitchen and we had to shout to be heard.

"Think of disappointment as a happy little surprise, Comfort. For instance . . ." Great-uncle Edisto pushed his glasses up on his nose and smiled like he had just invented a new thought. "I think I'll get me a nap." He was breathing hard. "There's always something good to come out of disappointment, Comfort. You'll see."

I could tell by the rhythm and tone of his voice that he was working up to his grand finale: "Open your arms to life! Let it strut into your heart in all its messy glory!"

"I don't like messes," I told him. "I like my plans."

Uncle Edisto patted me on the shoulder and lumbered off to his room. I called Declaration on the kitchen telephone, but her line was busy. I hung up and waited for her to call me, but she didn't, so I tried dialing her six more times. Then I gave up.

Tidings slammed the downstairs doors on his way back outside, and Dismay came to find me. We went to my closet to wait for something good to happen. I do my best thinking in the closet. It's quiet and comfortable and smells like opportunity. I sat with my back against the wall and my knees under my chin. Dismay sat facing me (it's a big closet), with his paws touching my bare toes. He panted nervously and his dog saliva drip-drip-dripped onto my feet.

"Thunder's gone," I said. "You can rest easy, boy."

Dismay wasn't sure, but he smiled at me anyway, with those shiny dog eyes. It made me want to hug him, so I did. His tail *thump-thump-thump*ed the floor.

The next thing I knew, Great-uncle Edisto surprised us all.

Great-great-aunt Florentine whooped for everyone to come. (Her bedroom was next to Great-uncle Edisto's bedroom, and she was standing at her mirror, she said later, soaking wet, untying the ribbon on her sunbonnet, when Great-uncle Edisto took his tumble.)

"It's an apoplexy!" she hollered. "Stroke!"

Everyone came running. We picked up Uncle

Edisto from where he had landed, put him into bed, covered him with one of Aunt Florentine's lavender-scented quilts, and called Doc MacRee. Mama sat on one side of Uncle Edisto's bed. She held Merry on her lap and looked exquisitely sad. Daddy kneeled next to Uncle Edisto on the other side of the bed and stroked his pale forehead. Tidings stood at attention next to Daddy, with his hand over his heart and a devastated look on his face.

Great-uncle Edisto gazed at us peacefully. He took us all in, like he was seeing us new, for the first time. His face was soft (turning a little gray), and, with the covers tucked under his chin, he looked for all the world like a small boy.

"Time to go home," he whispered. He blinked a slow blink, and when he opened his eyes, he seemed to be looking beyond us, to a land we couldn't see . . . a new world to explore.

"You *are* home, Uncle Edisto," I said. My heart pounded against my chest in a *Don't go! Don't go! Don't go!* beat. I kept one hand on Dismay; my dog stood next to me, calm and silent, keeping watch.

"You go on, Edisto," said Great-great-aunt Florentine, tears streaming down her wrinkled face. "It's your time. Have a wonderful trip, darlin'." She kissed him on the forehead and he closed his eyes. Then he smiled and . . . off he went.

I cried into Aunt Florentine's wet bosom. Everybody cried, because death is hard. Death is sad. But death is part of life. When someone you know dies, it's your job to keep on living.

So . . . we did. We adjusted. We did what we always do when death comes calling:

We gathered together.

We started cooking.

We called the relatives.

We called our friends.

We did not have to call the funeral home.

We *are* the funeral home.

I wrote the obituary.

Special to

THE AURORA COUNTY NEWS

(Mr. Johnson, this is for the March 28 twilight edition.)

Unexpected Death Comes Calling at Snowberger's!

Life Notices by Comfort Snowberger: Explorer, Recipe Tester, and Funeral Reporter

Imagine the shock and sadness all over Snapfinger, Mississippi, yesterday, when Edisto River Snowberger, patriarch of the Snowberger's Funeral Home Empire, died just before taking a nap after a failed picnic attempt due to a surprise thunderstorm. The entire Snowberger family sprang into action (that is, after we took a little time to sink into despair).

Edisto Snowberger was born in Fort Robinson, Nebraska, a stone's throw from the spot where Crazy Horse surrendered to General George

Crook (Discovering Our World Magazine, issue 72). He (Edisto) moved to Snapfinger with his favorite uncle, Allagash, to start a sawmill (Snapfinger being a town filled with piney woods). When the sawmill went kaput due to hard times and poor management, Edisto and Allagash looked around them and saw a town full of old folks sitting on sidewalk benches, swinging on front porches, and sleeping in church pews, and they said to each other, "What this town really needs is a funeral home."

So they started one in the old sawmill boardinghouse, which turned out to be a perfect funeral home house with its six bathrooms and two kitchens—one upstairs (for family meals) and one downstairs (for funeral flowers and funeral food storage). Thousands of dead people have come through Snowberger's and have ended up in either the "Rock of Ages" or the "Everlasting Arms" section of the Snapfinger Cemetery. Edisto Snowberger touched all their lives—and the lives of their families—with the greatest respect. To this very day, people look forward to dying and coming to Snowberger's for their laying out.

Edisto created the Snowberger family motto, "We Live to Serve," and Allagash engraved it on the Snowberger's Funeral Home sign. Edisto's sayings will be chronicled in the forthcoming book A Short History of a Small Place: Snapfinger, Mississippi, written by Comfort Snowberger. But that's another story.

Allagash died eons ago, and Edisto is survived by his uncle's wife, Florentine Snowberger, and the rest of the Snowberger clan, including especially his favorite niece, Comfort Snowberger, who was also his picnic companion.

Viewing will be at Snowberger's at 7pm on Wed. evening, and visitation will be at 2pm before the funeral at 3pm on Thurs. Bring your favorite picnic foods (and recipes), as we will spread blankets and cucumber sandwiches around the newly opened "Bread of Heaven" section of the Snapfinger Cemetery, where Edisto Snowberger will enter into his well-deserved eternal rest.

CHAPTER 2

Great-great-aunt Florentine died in that same vegetable garden where Uncle Edisto had his tomato mix-up. (It's a big garden.) It had been raining for days, but on that day, the sun was shining like a bright new penny. It was a Wednesday afternoon in September, just before Labor Day weekend. Everything (including school) in Snapfinger closes at noon on Wednesdays so everybody can go home, eat dinner early, and rest in the middle of the week. Of course, if your house is also the funeral home, you never really rest. You're always on call, just like the fire department is always on call. You never know when calamity will strike.

Great-great-aunt Florentine had been out hoeing in

the garden all morning, and she had ignored the noon whistle again, so Mama sent me out to tell her to come on in, the biscuits were getting cold. Dismay went with me, his black tail swishing and his tongue hanging out of his slobbery mouth: *I'm just so glad to be here!*

When we got to the edge of the garden where the zinnias are planted, there was Great-great-aunt Florentine, flat out on the ground next to a basket of crowder peas, with her garden dress poofed around her like a big, soft cloud and her head resting on a mound of marigolds. She was getting colder by the minute.

She had a serene look on her face. "Angelic," Mama later said. Her eyes were closed and she was smiling as if to say, *It's everything I'd hoped it would be, here in heaven! The streets are paved with lavender!*

Dismay sniffed at Great-great-aunt Florentine, then came back to stand with me. He licked my bare leg. I knew this was death—I'd seen it so many times before—and I knew what to do. I hugged Dismay first—he was so alive and full of good feelings—and I skedaddled for the house.

Everyone galloped out to the garden to gaze on Great-great-aunt Florentine. Bees buzzed around the bachelor's buttons that brushed up against Aunt Florentine's hip, but they did not touch her. I felt they were showing their respect. Dismay kept his distance, too. He looked up at me with that panting, dog-smiling mouth and those shiny black dog eyes: *What's happening? Is everything all right? Is it?* I gave him a reassuring pat, "It's okay, boy," and he settled down.

Daddy kneeled beside Great-great-aunt Florentine, crushing the bachelor's buttons (not to mention Aunt Florentine's hat). He held her wrist and put his ear to her chest. "Nothing," he said, looking at all of us as we crowded between the butter beans and the okra. "She's been here awhile . . ."

Mama nodded and looked grim—even grim looked beautiful on Mama. "Well . . . ," she said, "she was ninety-four years old, and she died doing what she wanted to be doing."

Tidings ran his fingers through his hair and gave his scalp a little scratch. "I'll bring the hearse around."

Now, Tidings is fourteen and too young to drive anything except the tractor, but Mama just said, "You do that, honey." Tidings and I exchanged a look—Mama knew. She knew that Tidings had been sneaking around and driving Daddy's old pickup through the cow pasture for the past year and a half. I shrugged. It's hard to pull one over on Mama.

Tidings saluted Mama and took off toward the funeral home garage. When he passed me, he tapped the brim of my hat twice.

Daddy stood, put his arm around Mama, and folded her to him. His voice wobbled. "She was ready to go, Joy." He rested his chin on the top of Mama's head, and they stood that way until Daddy said, "We've got the Hindman viewing at seven . . ."

Mama slipped her head out from under Daddy's chin, pulled his face down to hers, and kissed him firmly on his bearded cheek. "You'll be busy this afternoon, Bunch. We'll help." Then she reached for me and pulled me into the embrace, so the three of us stood together like one giant statue-headstone in a vegetable-garden cemetery, guarding the temporary graveside of Great-great-aunt Florentine and brushing up against the tomatoes. It felt good.

My parents smell like a mixture of gardenias and embalming fluid, even in the evenings after their showers. I think the smells of their jobs have permanently soaked into their skins. I don't mind. I'm used to how they smell. I rested in that familiar odor while the sun baked my back. Dismay rubbed his shaggy side against us and sniffed at us.

“Comfort,” Mama said, “I’m going to need your help in the flower shop.”

My heart made a little *poof* in my chest. I’d made plans to go cloud watching with Declaration. Declaration had spent the entire summer in Mobile with her mama’s kin (a first), and we hadn’t had an overnight or a good visit for ice ages. I’d been asking her to meet me at Listening Rock for three weekends straight, ever since school had started again, and finally, she’d said she could. And finally, there was no rain.

And now I wasn’t going to show up.

But death doesn’t respect plans or the weather—that much I knew. And Declaration would know where to find me. So I didn’t even protest out loud; I just squared my shoulders, looked Mama in the eye, and said in my most sincere voice, “I live to serve.” She smiled at me.

Merry had lagged behind the rest of us. She had been distracted by the squash plants. (They were blooming again from a late summer planting.) She had been picking the tender squash blossoms and sticking them to her cheeks until she was festooned with them. When she discovered Great-great-aunt Florentine, she sat on her with a *thump*. She slanted her short self in the direction of Aunt Florentine's face and stared intently into her closed eyes.

"Dead!" Merry said.

"Yes," said Mama. She gathered Merry into her arms.

Once again, I wrote the obituary.

Special to

THE AURORA COUNTY NEWS

(Mr. Johnson, this is for
the September 4 early afternoon edition.)

Yet Another Untimely Death at Snowberger's!!!

Life Notices by Comfort Snowberger: Explorer, Recipe Tester, and Funeral Reporter

Grab your handkerchiefs! Eggs Florentine Snowberger, matriarch of the Snowberger's Funeral Home Empire, has died at the ripe old age of 94 after a long and (extremely) colorful life.

She was born into a chicken-farming family, the Petersons, of Halleluia, Mississippi. Her older brother, Benedict, moved to nearby Snapfinger to work at Snowberger's Sawmill when it opened, and that's how Florentine, while visiting Benedict, met Allagash. They fell in love, married, and moved into the old sawmill boardinghouse that became Snowberger's Funeral Home. It's a long story and too much to go into here.

Today the entire Snowberger family lives above Snowberger's Funeral Home in more rooms than this reporter can count. Florentine decorated every room with lavender (her signature herb) and made it her business to sample all funeral food on funeral days. With her favorite niece, Comfort Snowberger, she was compiling a cookbook called Fantastic (and Fun) Funeral Food for Family and Friends.

Some people (we won't name names) said Florentine Snowberger was a gossip, but she called herself a geographer. She studied the earth (Snapfinger, especially) and life on the earth (Snapfinger, particularly) and figured out how life on the earth affected the earth (Snapfinger, notably). She passed on her love of geography to her niece Comfort and willed to her (long before she died) all her old copies of Discovering Our

World Magazine. This generous gift has directly influenced Comfort's decision to become an explorer when she grows up.

The viewing will be at 7pm on Fri., Sept. 4. The funeral will be at 4pm on Sat., Sept. 5, with visitation for an hour before the service. It's Labor Day weekend, but don't let that stop you. Y'all loved Florentine Snowberger as much as we did, and (as Florentine always said) a funeral offers the perfect time to study geography. So get in the car and come on to the funeral . . . unless your name is Peach Shuggars. We do not want a repeat of what happened at Edisto Snowberger's funeral—so if your name is Peach Shuggars, stay home, stay home, stay home! I cannot stress this enough. Stay home. Stay. Home. You hear me?

Snowberger's Funeral Home

RURAL ROUTE 2, SNAPFINGER, MISSISSIPPI

Typed on Daddy's Royal typewriter
at 3:27 pm on Wed., Sept. 2

Declaration Johnson
8309 Magnolia Street
Snapfinger, Mississippi

Dear Best Friend Declaration,

By now you have figured out that I didn't show up at Listening Rock to meet you, and you are back home wondering if I got run over, flat as a pancake, by a corn harvester out of control on County Road 2435. Well, no.

I have a sad surprise for you: Great-great-aunt Florentine is dead. Can you believe it? She dropped down in the garden, like a leaf tumbling off the oak tree of life, just before I was supposed to meet you at Listening Rock.

I won't go to school for the next two days,

but Mama says I can meet you at 3pm on Fri. at Listening Rock. I will bring a picnic.

Aunt Florentine's funeral is at 4pm on Sat. I know you said, after attending Great-uncle Edisto's funeral, that you would forevermore stop going to funerals, but I hope you'll make an exception for this one.

Please send word back through your daddy and let me know if you can come on Fri.

Sincerely, as ever, herewith and forever Your Best Friend,

Comfort Snowberger
Explorer, Recipe Tester,
and Funeral Reporter
Rural Route 2
Snapfinger, Mississippi

Dear Comfort,

Fine.

Declaration

CHAPTER 3

For two whole days, we Snowbergers were busy. Daddy worked on Great-great-aunt Florentine and made her beautiful in her alabaster-white casket. Tidings sat, tall and straight, on the tractor—as determined as General Sherman marching through Georgia—and cut the grass between rain showers. Merry sang songs—all to the tune of "Jingle Bells"—and took little catnaps on a pink blanket under the pecan tree by the downstairs kitchen door. She would fall asleep snoring against Dismay, who would thump his long black tail with happiness.

Mama and Tidings and I cut flowers so Mama could fill orders in her shop from all the neighbors who had called to send bouquets. Lurleen, Mama's helper, came to help arrange them. Then Mama and I cooked six tuna casseroles six different ways, and we baked four chocolate cakes and dusted them with confectioners' sugar. "Aunt Florentine's favorites . . . ," said Mama. We cleaned Aunt Florentine's room so it would be in order, forever.

In Aunt Florentine's nightstand we found a picture of Declaration and me when we were four years old. We were wearing matching red pajamas and laughing at the camera.

"That was the Christmas after Declaration's mama died," said Mama. "Aunt Florentine sewed those pajamas herself."

"I remember," I said.

Mama and I stared at the picture until the grandfather clock in the hallway bonged and we both sniffed. "Go on and make your picnic," she said. "You have served enough for today. Tell Declaration we miss her."

"Yes, ma'am!" I headed for the kitchen.

Now, I hadn't spoken to Declaration since Aunt Florentine's death. For some reason she hadn't come by the house at all on the day Aunt Florentine died, but her daddy, Mr. Plas Johnson, who is a friend and fishing partner of my daddy's, came by that afternoon to pay his respects and talk to Daddy about the obituary for Great-great-aunt Florentine.

Mr. Johnson owns the *Aurora County News,* and he always writes the obituaries himself. He needs help, in my opinion. He puts the obituaries under a column he calls "Death Notices," so of course they are written in a deadly dull and unexciting way, although I would never tell him that. Great-great-aunt Florentine would hoot over Mr. Johnson's obituaries. She'd say things like, "I could tell you *all* about Lyle Latham, but nobody asks me!" She's the one who said, "*Death* doesn't notice anything! *Life* notices everything! Write *Life Notices,* Comfort!" So I do.

I feel that my Life Notices are much more colorful and interesting than Mr. Johnson's Death Notices, but that's just a matter of opinion—and it's his newspaper. Still, he says he will print my obituaries if I can make them "newspaper worthy," whatever that means. "Just the facts, Comfort," he always tells me.

When Mr. Johnson and Daddy were done, I gave Mr. Johnson my Life Notice for Aunt Florentine, and I also gave him a letter for Declaration. Declaration's note back to me was prickly, bordering on peevish. So, because it was Friday and picnic time, I made Declaration her favorite kind of tuna-fish sandwich. I added hard-boiled eggs and apples and dill pickle slices. Declaration loved Great-great-aunt Florentine's pickles. We'd first eaten them together at Snowberger's on the day we met, which was on the day of Declaration's mama's funeral (death by illness). I had gone downstairs to the funeral like I always did. That didn't seem unusual to Declaration then, when we were four, but a while back she had started remarking (for instance): "You're not even related to the Dapplevines!"

But I *was,* according to Great-uncle Edisto. After the funeral he had taken me and Declaration on our first picnic together. We'd eaten tuner-fish sandwiches. And right then and there, Declaration and I had decided to be best friends. She didn't have brothers and sisters, and she liked my house, where there was lots of family. When she slept over, Declaration and I always lay with Great-great-aunt Florentine in her big bed. Declaration would talk about her mama and cry into a Snowberger's handkerchief. Aunt Florentine and I were good listeners because we were used to death. We lived with it.

I packed our picnic in my backpack, then ran down the stairs and out the back door, whistling for Dismay. I grabbed my bike and ran alongside it until I could jump on. I pedaled hard down Rural Route 2, past the cornfield, then turned left onto County Road 2435. The cemetery was up a slope to my left, and Purgatory Hill plunged down to the oak grove on my right. It was my favorite part of the ride. I turned off the road onto Purgatory Hill. I steadied the pedals with my feet and steered myself down the hill, bumping and weaving to the bottom.

I didn't see Declaration anywhere. Usually we timed ourselves so well that we met each other as we got to the bottom of Purgatory Hill. I waited for a minute, but Dismay was barking from somewhere inside the grove, calling me to *Come climb this rock!* So I did. Declaration could find me at the top. I'd watch for her. I parked my bike against the first oak tree I came to and ran into the woody grove to find my dog.

Chapter 4

The oak grove was gnat-filled and steamy in late summer, but it was a paradise of grasses, acorns, pinecones, sandy spots, and rocks to climb, not to mention squirrels, rabbits, foxes, and mice for Dismay to chase. Creatures great and small lived together in the grove, hidden under a leafy oak canopy. Snapfinger Creek trickled its way through the trees. The oak grove was Snapfinger's most unsung treasure. I felt alive there.

So did my dog. Dismay was beside himself with joy—living things! Air! Trees! He made friends with every tree he came to—I never knew one dog could pee so often or so much. I caught up with him at the base of Listening Rock, where he slurped his sloppy tongue all over my face in a frenzied *Hurry up!,* his breath smelling like lima beans. I buried my face in his shaggy neck and hugged him. "Good dog!" I whispered.

I made one last look-around for Declaration—no, not yet—then Dismay and I made our way to the top of Listening Rock.

A thick stand of rose of Sharon bushes guarded the path with strong woody branches full of wide pink blooms. Hummingbirds and butterflies nosed around the sweet scent. I gave an appreciative sniff as I walked past the sentries and entered the world of Listening Rock.

I had to watch my footing, but mostly the walk to the top was an easy one, even in my black flip-flops, and I often imagined myself as Meriwether Lewis on the Lewis and Clark expedition (*Discovering Our World Magazine,* issue 14), hiking up an enormous boulder worn smooth by what Uncle Edisto said was thousands of years of water flowing over and around Listening Rock in the ice ages. "Granite and slate," he said each time we visited, "maybe a little soapstone, sprinkled with limestone and quartz. Minerals galore! It's a smorgasbord of metamorphic marvels!"

It was. Listening Rock glittered where the quartz sparkled it. It pebbled and flaked in the limestone places. Here and there scrub pines and bushes jutted from the granite surface. Patches of daisies sprouted from the rock in sandy places, with a few determined bumblebees buzzing around them, but mostly there was wide, warm rock to walk on at a slow but steady rise.

It took about the time it takes to eat a tuna-fish sandwich to get to the top. There, the surface was about the size of Snowberger's big front parking lot, only, unlike the Snowberger's lot, the top of Listening Rock gently rolled and sloped. The gnats that were fierce down in the grove didn't bother us at the top of Listening Rock; the breeze kept them away from our faces.

Dismay stood, majestic, washed in sunlight, near the edge of the rock, on the tip-top of the slope, like he always did when he first got there. Regally he blinked at his dogdom, sniffing at the high air. The oak grove waved its leafy green flags at us, shouting, "Hail, Dismay!" A little farther out, across Snapfinger Creek and County Road 2435, the headstones in the Snapfinger Cemetery stood guard against all enemies like soft, silent sentries. Just beyond the cornfield was Snowberger's, its tidy white fence holding a tiny kingdom safe within its arms—with the old sawmill boardinghouse that was my home rising up like a castle in the countryside. Rural Route 2 was dotted with pickup trucks meandering toward the towns of Snapfinger and Halleluia, Bay Springs and Puckett.

I'd wrapped Declaration's sandwich in two pieces of waxed paper so it wouldn't go stale; the paper made a crinkling sound as I set the sandwich in the best flat spot. I had two Royal Crown Colas in glass bottles. RC Cola was Declaration's favorite. Dismay had exhausted himself chasing rabbits and chewing up sticks. Soon he was snoring in a shady spot under a fat juniper bush that spread out from a rock crevasse.

Everything was ready. I lay on my back, closed my eyes, pulled my Snowberger's baseball cap over my face, and listened to the sound of Listening Rock baking in the sun. I wondered if Great-great-aunt Florentine could hear the blue jay I heard calling. Maybe she could. But she would never feel the warm sunshine on her face again. Tears gathered in the corners of my eyes, and I mopped at them with my fingers.

"Dying is a transition, Comfort, that's all," Great-uncle Edisto used to say.

"A transition to what?" I'd ask. "What's next?"

"Who knows?" Uncle Edisto would say. "But life's

not a line, Comfort; it's a circle. Just look around you and you'll see that."

I sat up and looked around me. It was September. Uncle Edisto had died in March. It seemed like a million ice ages had gone by since he'd left us for whatever adventure was next. An oak leaf drifted lazily in the breeze. As I watched it make its way to earth, I spotted Declaration coming up the rock. Finally! Dismay thumped his tail as if, even asleep, he knew Declaration was there.

I stood, waved to Declaration, and said, "Hey!" She looked up and gave a short wave with a gloved hand but said nothing. Up and up she came. Her footfalls slapped Listening Rock and her breath puffed her cheeks in and out. As she got closer, I could see the ribbons on her hat, the buttons on her sundress, and her painted toenails in her sandals as she gained the top of Listening Rock and stood in front of me. She had a beach towel folded under her arm. Her face was a sweaty pomegranate red. I smiled my biggest smile at her.

She didn't smile back.

Uncle Edisto always said, "The heart hears more than the ear." My heart listened as it thumped in my chest.

My smile wavered. "Declaration?"

Chapter 5

Declaration took a breath and made a *Whoosh!* sound through her teeth. It made her lips flap. She raised her eyebrows in a look that said, I made it! And finally, she smiled at me. My heart stopped thumping, and I felt a flood of relief through my chest that tickled my throat and made me laugh. I rested my hands on my bare knees while I laughed, but I kept my eyes on Declaration. "I'm so glad to see you!"

That made Declaration laugh, too. Her curls bounced under her hat. She walked past me and flapped out her towel. It floated like a magic carpet into the thick September air and settled perfectly onto

Listening Rock, as it always did. She sat down carefully, as she always did. She took off her sandals and placed them neatly beside her towel . . . just the way she always did.

Declaration *dressed* for every occasion, even for a picnic. I always wore my lime green shorts, my Snowberger's baseball shirt, and my Snowberger's baseball cap. I liked knowing what I was going to wear. That meant I could use my deciding powers on other things.

Dismay gave a sleeping snort. His long legs moved like he was running in a dream.

"Oh, *Comfort*!" Declaration complained, weaving a gloved hand back and forth in Dismay's general direction.

"I know, I know," I said, sitting down. "But he's been cooped up at home for the last two days, and he needs to get out as much as I do. Look—he's all spent!"

Declaration made a face. "Fine." She kept her gaze on the Snapfinger Cemetery, where a great hum had started. Old Johnny Mercer was chewing up the earth with a backhoe.

I handed Declaration an RC Cola and I gestured toward Old Johnny. "He's digging Great-great-aunt Florentine's grave."

Declaration nodded. She took the RC with gloved hands, removed the cap, and with a small smile of thanks, drank a sip.

I licked my lips and watched her. "Want a sandwich?" I asked. "I brought 'tuner-fish'!"

"No, thank you . . . *Uncle Edisto.*"

"Pickle?"

"No!" The skin between Declaration's eyebrows wrinkled up—she looked like she was thinking about what she wanted to say next but couldn't quite come up with it.

I tried to help. "I can't remember the last time I saw you . . ."

"You just saw me at school on Wednesday!"

". . . on top of Listening Rock," I finished.

Declaration let out a long sigh. She picked a pine needle off her dress.

I scratched at a mosquito bite on my ankle. "Are you mad at me?"

"No." She took off her hat and smoothed her hair away from her face. "Why?"

"Your note was awful persnickety."

"Was it?" Declaration fanned herself with her hat and spoke in a lofty tone. "I was in a rush when I wrote it—sorry."

"Oh." I wanted to believe her. I changed the subject. "I have so much to tell you!"

Declaration glanced at me and reached for her sandals. "I can't stay."

I scrambled to my feet. "Why not?"

A silent Declaration pulled on one sandal at a time.

I stood in front of her. "You're mad because I didn't show up on Wednesday! It couldn't be helped!" My stomach had that sour feeling to it, like I'd eaten an entire bag of raw peanuts. "You had to wait too long . . . I'm sorry about that . . . But if you could have seen Aunt Florentine . . . Even Daddy got choked up . . ."

"Stop!" Declaration took a big gulp of her RC and put her hat back on her head. Then, as if she had fortified herself and come to a decision, she said, "I didn't wait."

"Oh!" I adjusted my hat on my head. "Why not?"

Declaration pursed her lips. "I didn't come."

"Oh . . ." I sat down. The sun was directly in my eyes, so I put my hand up and under my baseball cap, like a salute, and I squinted in Declaration's direction. "Why not?" When she didn't answer me, I asked, "Did something tragic happen to you, too?"

Declaration's face pinked up. She kept her eyes on her shoes. "No."

Old Johnny Mercer's backhoe bucket clanged and dropped dirt into a big pile next to Great-great-aunt Florentine's grave. Dismay snored on.

"Well . . . why, then, Declaration? Why didn't you come?"

Declaration shrugged. "I can't say."

The back of my throat stung with tears. "You haven't been to my house all summer . . ."

"I was in Mobile!"

"And then I had to pester you at school to meet me at Listening Rock—and then you didn't even bother to come when you said you would!"

"I'm here now!"

"You haven't even called me! Aunt Florentine died!"

Declaration shook her head. She wouldn't look at me. "You don't understand . . ."

"Well, then, what is it?" I made myself listen to my breathing so I wouldn't cry.

"Maybe I just don't like . . . some things . . . anymore . . . like this sorry old rock."

I stared at Declaration as hard as I could, and she added, "It gives my feet blisters when I climb it!" She stuck her chin out and continued in a serious tone.

"My grandmother Lucy says a lady doesn't climb rocks after a certain age. She says my mother would be *scandalized* to think of me climbing rocks or playing kickball in my school dresses at recess!"

Now, I've met Grandmother Lucy. She's at least 480 years old. She is always giving Declaration advice from the Dark Ages that doesn't make any sense to me. Now that Declaration had spent a whole summer with Grandmother Lucy and all her mama's relatives, I'd have to wait a long time for all the latest advice to wear off.

I looked at Dismay, so happy to be on top of Listening Rock, sleeping. As he breathed, his nostrils expanded and contracted and his nose glistened, cold and wet in the warm, sunshiny September afternoon. I wished he'd wake up and come sit by me.

"Well, then," I said, "why are you here, Declaration?"

Declaration sighed. "I came to pay my respects, of course." She handed me her empty RC bottle. "I'm sorry about Aunt Florentine. I'm . . . I'm real sad about it." Her voice gargled in her throat. She twirled one of her curls around and around one finger. "I decided to come here to pay my respects since I'm not coming to the funeral."

"Don't say that, Declaration." I swallowed my tears. "I knew you would say that . . ."

Declaration fidgeted on her towel. "You know I hate funerals—they depress me."

Now, the only funeral she'd ever been to other than her mother's was Great-uncle Edisto's. "I know," I said quickly, using my helpful voice. "I asked Aunt Florentine about it once, Declaration—she said Uncle Edisto's funeral had been upsetting to you because it put you in mind of your mama and her death. She reminded me that you hadn't talked about your mama for ice ages!"

Declaration studied her sandaled feet, as if she were looking for blisters. Then she said, "I heard a lot of stories about my mama this summer. I had a good time in Mobile." She pursed her lips again. "Maybe I'll move there."

"No, you won't," I said, as if I was the boss of Declaration. "Will you?"

Declaration shrugged. "Probably not. At least not for now." We sat in silence for a while, and then Declaration said, "I can't remember what Mama looked like anymore, until I see a picture of her." She wiped at her eyes.

I wanted to be helpful, and I didn't want Declaration to move—ever. "You just need to go to more funerals, Declaration, that'll take care of that. I mean . . . look at me. You get used to death if you live around it long enough."

Declaration shook her head. "Don't you think it's strange that you go to so many funerals, Comfort?"

"No. But I *would* think it was strange if you didn't come to Aunt Florentine's funeral—you were a member of our family to her!"

Declaration studied Old Johnny Mercer putting a green tarp over Aunt Florentine's grave site. She was composing herself. She didn't like to act emotional in front of anybody. Her grandmother Lucy had told her that a lady never sneezes, burps, runs, screams, or cries in public. Which made me think about Peach.

"And I really need you to come," I said, "because Peach is coming, and you know what that means!"

"Then I *know* I'm not coming!" said Declaration. At Great-uncle Edisto's funeral, Peach had thrown up into a potted fern and then had dribbled vomit on Declaration's new patent-leather shoes. She had screamed at him, which was what made him run outside and fling himself into the azaleas.

"Oh, please, Declaration! Not even for me?" The stinging place in my throat had turned into a big lump.

"He's not *my* cousin." Declaration stood up.

So did I. "Aunt Florentine loved you as much as she loved me." I swallowed hard and spoke the truth. My tears came, along with the memories. "She taught you how to make cherry cobbler. She braided your hair when you spent the night . . . and she listened to all your stories about your mama . . ." I wiped at my face.

Declaration's eyes filled with tears, too. She smoothed the front of her sundress, picked up her towel, and with careful hands rolled it into a ball. She dabbed at her eyes with her towel. Then she sniffed and said, "Fine."

"Really?" I hardly dared to believe her.

"Yes." Declaration looked me in the eye. She gave a small shudder. "Grandmother Lucy says, 'A lady always honors her societal obligations, no matter how it ruins her more pleasant plans.' Daddy wants me to go, but he told me it's my choice."

She tucked her towel under one arm and gave me a flat smile. "So, fine—I'll come." She pointed a finger at me. "But I'm not coming to the viewing tonight, and I'm not getting anywhere near Peach tomorrow—just so you know. I had to get new shoes after Uncle Edisto's funeral! Don't expect me to spend one minute with Peach!"

"I won't," I said. "I promise . . ."

Dismay groaned. He opened his eyes, wobbled to his feet, stretched a long stretch, and shook himself all over, slowly, as if he were coming back alive. He wagged his tail at the sight of Declaration. She pointed a gloved finger at Dismay. "Don't you dare, dog . . . This is a new dress."

Dismay sat down and panted at Declaration in his calm dog way. It was the respectful way he sat with the grieving when he was on duty at funerals. Folks appreciated Dismay's presence at Snowberger's. They knew that he had slept all night next to their loved one's casket, on the night before the funeral. It was Dismay's way of seeing them off to the next world. He kept a vigil.

"Dismay isn't just any dog," I said. "If you would only hug him once, you'd see. He's full of good feelings—and they sink right into you when you hug him."

"No, thanks," said Declaration. "I've got to go . . . Daddy's expecting me back soon."

"Could you spend the night tonight?"

Declaration shook her head. "I can't tonight." She didn't give me a reason why; she just began making her way down Listening Rock. She didn't even say good-bye.

"Don't forget, the funeral's at four!" I called after her. "Visitation's at three!"

The sun had shifted lower on the horizon, and long shadows began to creep across the Snapfinger Cemetery. In the distance Old Johnny Mercer had finished setting up the large green tarp over Aunt Florentine's grave site. It looked like a circus tent, open on all sides, with SNOWBERGER'S painted in bright white letters across the top of one side and WE LIVE TO SERVE on the other. If we had rain the next day, or if the sun was blistering hot, we would all be under the green tarp together, saying good-bye to Aunt Florentine.

I heard a crinkling sound and turned my head toward it. Dismay was chewing hard, in great big chomps. Waxed paper dangled from his jaws. He smiled at me as he chewed. It was a good sandwich. Especially the extra pickles.

"You *dog,* you!"

Dismay chomped faster.

I laughed at my dog—and at my own joke. Then I lay flat on my back for a few minutes and watched a cloud turn into Abraham Lincoln's hat, which made me think of Great-uncle Edisto and his tomatoes. I ate my tuner-fish sandwich.

I felt a whole lot better after that. Now I needed to get home before Peach showed up.

Special to

The Aurora County News

(Mr. Johnson, please print this whenever you've got a slow news day.)

Top Ten Tips for First-rate Funeral Behavior

Life Notices and Tips by Comfort Snowberger: Explorer, Recipe Tester, and Funeral Reporter

1. You don't have to wear black to a funeral. Any old color is fine; just don't wear a wedding dress or your torn shorts. No bare feet or flip-flops. Comb your hair. The deceased (a fancy word for the person who died) will wear more makeup than all the mourners combined; so if you run out of time getting ready to come to the funeral, don't worry about makeup.

2. Let's talk about the deceased. The deceased lies, all dressed up, in the open casket (which

is a nice word for a coffin), with his hair combed better than he ever combed it when he was alive. During the viewing, which happens the day before the funeral, people wander up to the open casket and stare at the deceased and say things like, "He looks so natural," which is silly, because he doesn't look natural—he looks dead. But that's okay; he's supposed to be dead. But don't say, "He looks so dead"; that's not a good idea. Some people are queasy about looking at the deceased. Don't worry about it. He doesn't mind.

3. A visitation, which happens right before the funeral, is a time for folks to visit the family and to offer them comfort. The casket is closed during the visitation; so if you don't want to see your dead one laid out in the open casket, just come to the visitation and not the viewing. People who come to the viewing, visitation, and funeral are called the mourners (that's you). The folks who are related to the person who died are called the family. (They are also mourners.)

In Snapfinger this can be most of the folks in town. Be nice to the family and talk to them. At the viewing they are usually standing next to the open casket (where the deceased is lying) in the Serenity Suite and wishing the deceased would sit up and talk with them, but of course the deceased isn't talking, so you have to do the talking. Here's what to say to the family during the viewing, visitation, and funeral time: "I'm so sorry." That's all. Then move on. Don't say, "He's gone to a better place," or "You must be relieved," or "That shirt doesn't go with those pants."

4. This is not a good time to remind the family that the deceased owes you money.

5. You will find boxes of Kleenex stationed all around the visitation room. At Snowberger's, there are also handkerchiefs available. Don't fake your crying like some folks do—it's impolite and people can tell. On the other hand, don't genuinely sob so much that you call attention to yourself (you

know who you are). The visitation is also a good time for laughing and remembering funny stories about the deceased. A visitation is sort of like a sad party, with the deceased being the center of attention.

6. Take all arguments and fistfights outside to the parking lot.

7. Here's the order of events on the day of the funeral: One: Visitation at the funeral home for an hour before the funeral service. Two: Funeral service at the funeral home. Three: After the funeral service everybody gets into their cars and drives, in a long line, to the cemetery. (You can walk it, but nobody feels like walking on a funeral day.) Four: Then there's a graveside service at the Snapfinger Cemetery. Go to the bathroom before you get in your car to go to the cemetery, in case Preacher Powell gets long-winded at the cemetery.

8. Order flowers from Snowberger's Flowers next door, and they'll be at the funeral home

before you are, where they'll dress up the Serenity Suite. The family appreciates it (they don't feel like decorating at a time like this), and they'll keep the little cards of sympathy that come with the flowers. All the visitors (that's you) will walk around in the Serenity Suite and read the cards that come with the flowers, to see whose flowers are the prettiest, whose are the biggest, whose are the best smelling. It's kind of like a contest. If you don't send flowers, everybody will notice. Don't send balloons or candy or presents. This isn't a birthday party; it's a funeral. Just send flowers.

9. Bring a covered dish of food with you to the funeral home. At Snowberger's there is always a covered-dish dinner back at the funeral home after the graveside service. Favorite dishes: chicken casseroles and Jell-O molds of all colors and descriptions, anything with mandarin oranges in it, Vienna sausage and Ritz cracker trays, pimiento-cheese sandwiches (cut into triangles), and dog treats for Dismay, Funeral

Dog Extraordinaire. Nobody eats the asparagus or brussels sprouts, and I don't know why folks would bring those to a covered-dish supper (unless they're just so depressed that they need to bring depressing food). So those of you who bring these unpopular dishes, please stop. Also, just a gustatory note (as Florentine Snowberger would say)—you can never have too many brownies. Bring your recipes, too. The recipes for all these dishes and more will be printed in the forthcoming Fantastic (and Fun) Funeral Food for Families and Friends by Florentine and Comfort Snowberger.

10. Remember that death is a natural thing—it's all around us, as Edisto Snowberger always said. Don't try to hide death from kids. If Grandpa has died, don't say, "We lost Grandpa," because little kids will want to know why you don't go look for him. Just say, "Grandpa died." Don't say, "Grandpa passed," either, because we'll wonder what grade he was in. Just say he died. We get it. Kids are better at death than grown-ups

give them credit for, unless the kid is Peach Shuggars. Discourage Peach Shuggars from coming to your funeral. Discourage Peach Shuggars from visiting Snapfinger, Mississippi. Discourage Peach, <u>period.</u>

CHAPTER 6

Dismay and I went home the way we'd come. It had rained for so many days that Snapfinger Creek had swollen to a good-sized stream. Dismay twirled and splashed in it, cooling himself.

I walked my bike to the shade of a chokecherry tree and watched my dog. The ground was spongy, and my toes felt deliciously wet and cool in my flip-flopped feet. When Dismay spotted me watching him, he plopped himself down in the creek, just like that. The water came to his shoulders and almost covered his back, so that he looked like a dog-headed Viking ship on a mighty river. He looked at me with bright black eyes, his pink tongue hanging out of his mouth, and a panting grin that said, *Come on!*

"Come out of there, Dismay!" I called to him. "We've got to get home!" Right out of the water he came, friendly and happy. As soon as he got close to me, he gave himself a giant shake and peppered me with Snapfinger Creek water.

"Dis*may*!" I shouted. He barked, and wagged his tail, and I had to laugh. "Let's go!"

I avoided any possibility of seeing my cousin Peach as we traveled home. Whenever I heard a car coming, I steered my bike smack into the cornfield and let the corn silks tickle me while I waited for it to pass. Dismay thought this was a good game, and he squeezed right in with me, knocking me into cornstalks, sniffing for rabbits as he pushed himself into each row. He was a good corn trampler.

I hatched a plan as I pedaled into the front parking lot. I would go right to my closet. I wouldn't go to the family supper before the viewing—in fact, I'd skip the viewing, too. That way I wouldn't have to see Peach at all until the next day. I'd fortify myself with a stack of peanut-butter-and-banana sandwiches and my notebooks for *A Short History of a Small Place.* (I called it

Short for short.) I put all my Life Notices into *Short,* and also my "funeral geography," as Aunt Florentine called it—notes about who came to each funeral and what folks said and whose food they didn't eat. Ever since I could write, I've kept a record of every funeral I've attended—I've been to 247. Great-great-aunt Florentine would be number 248.

Yes, the closet. That's where I needed to be.

CHAPTER 7

Mama was walking across the freshly mowed grass from the funeral home to the flower shop when she saw me snake past the corner of the shed. "Comfort!" she called. She waved a gloved hand at me like she was the beauty queen of the garden club. Her smile made the air shine. "I need you!"

Mama said something else, but her words were drowned out by Tidings, riding the tractor back toward the shed. He had his shirt off and his fishing boots on. He glistened with sweat and was concentrating like he was Michelangelo sculpting the statue of David (*Discovering Our World Magazine,* issue 47). Dismay ran in front of the mower, barking and spinning.

"Give him some water from the hose!" I yelled at Tidings.

"Give him a bath!" Mama called. "He's working tonight!"

Tidings saluted us. Mama disappeared inside the shop, and I followed her. She smiled at me with teary eyes and gestured around the shop.

Lavender. It was everywhere. Great-great-aunt Florentine had stuffed lavender sprigs in her pockets and in her pillows, in her drawers, in her hair—she had been a walking lavender bush.

"I've been cutting and arranging lavender all day!" said Mama, dabbing at her eyes with a Snowberger's handkerchief. "Oh, it brings back memories! Sweet memories. Your aunt Florentine would have loved all this, wouldn't she?" She sniffed a ladylike sniff and quickly stuck her handkerchief into a pocket.

Before I could think of what to say, Mama picked up florist wire, kitchen shears, and a bucket of pink tea roses and scooted past me. "Can you help me tote these buckets of flowers next door? I'll arrange them in the downstairs kitchen. Lurleen can't get here to help me for another hour, and I've got more orders than I can shake a stick at."

"I live to serve," I said valiantly.

Mama looked right into my eyes and smiled a genuine smile that showed all the sadness around her mouth and behind her eyes. It made me love her a lot.

Mama was the picture of poise. She had been "Little Miss Magnolia" of Aurora County when she was six years old, and she was the most beautiful homecoming queen Snapfinger High School had ever seen—folks still said so. She made a florist apron full of pockets look like a regal robe, with presents peeking out for everyone. She put her armful of supplies into an enormous red wagon that sat in the middle of the shop. It was brimming with buckets of orange lilies, purple stock, yellow spray roses, red carnations, baby snapdragons . . . and lavender, lavender, lavender.

"Merry's taking a nap in the casket room, so we'll want to be quiet when we pass her. She's all worn out," Mama said.

I envisioned Merry curled up inside an empty open casket, lying on smooth white satin and clutching her blanket to herself, snoring her little-girl snores. "Why is she in there?"

Mama pulled on a pair of gloves. "Well, your aunt Florentine can't watch her anymore on funeral days, of course, so I've got to keep her close while I work. Maybe you can play with her when she wakes up . . ." She reached for a bunch of baby's breath.

"Oh, *Mama* . . ."

"Just make her a peanut-butter-and-banana sandwich and let her play in the dress-up box. She'll be plenty happy." Mama kissed me on the nose. Everything Mama did felt like it had great purpose to it, even a kiss on the nose. "And when Lurleen comes, she'll bring Jimmie, and Jimmie can watch Merry while she helps in the kitchen—deal?"

A nose-kiss had sealed the deal.

"Can I skip the viewing tonight?" I asked, as together we balanced the buckets and hauled the wagon across the yard to the funeral home.

"That's not like you." Mama caught a giant magenta clump that tumbled from the wagon. "Isn't this the most glorious celosia? My gardens have been beautiful this year, even with all the rain." Celosia reminded me of enormous celery stalks with a mass of red brains on top.

"I have a lot of homework," I said.

Now, I didn't have a lot of homework, but I'd find some if it meant I didn't have to see Peach. I love homework. I do homework when I don't have any homework to do. It's calming to read about Egypt and then to draw up your own plan for a pyramid just because you feel like it. I had recently drawn a map of Snowberger's, just because.

Mama tucked the celosia stalk under her arm. "You don't want to see Peach." She wore a straw hat that protected her face from the sun. She looked at me with her head cocked to the right, her eyebrows raised, and that half smile she wore when she knew she was right.

I sighed and wiped my hands on my lime green shorts. "Yes, ma'am . . ."

"I can't say as I blame you." Mama went back to work, pulling the wagon across the grass carpet. I pushed. "But he won't come to the viewing," she said. "After supper we'll put him to bed downstairs in the resting room, like we did when Uncle Edisto died, and he'll sleep right through it."

The resting room was next to Daddy's office. It's where folks had a little lie-down if they got overwrought during a viewing or a visitation (it happened), and it's where Daddy napped if he got tired during the day. It held two twin beds and a nightstand between them; nothing else. It was a good, simple room.

"Peach won't even know you're there," said Mama.

"Yes, he will," I said. "He'll see me at supper, and then he'll pester me all night!" I put on my best tinny, puny, scrawny Peach voice—" *'Comfort! My drink's too cold!' 'Comfort! I need my softer pajamas!' 'Comfort! This story is too scary!'* "—and then I went back to my own voice. "And you'll make me stay with him and play crazy eights in the resting room all evening, and I'll miss the whole viewing . . . Like you said, Great-great-aunt Florentine can't help anymore . . ."

"You know," said Mama, "he adores you, Comfort, he always has—"

"I don't want to be adored!"

"—and he's lost the people he adored most."

Whenever Peach and Aunt Goldie visited us from Atlanta (which was too often), Peach would race into Uncle Edisto's arms, overjoyed, shouting (depending on the occasion), "It's *Easter* and I've come to *see* you!" And Uncle Edisto would catch Peach and swing him high (before his arthritis got too bad) and say, "Well, come see me, then!" After Uncle Edisto died, Peach shouted the same thing to Aunt Florentine. "It's *summer* and I've come to *see* you!" She'd fold him into her apron, wrapping him in a cloud of lavender, and say the same thing—"Well, come see me, then!" And Peach would cry from happiness.

"Death is hard for Peach," Mama said. "He's only eight . . ."

"Oh, *Mama*! I went to funerals when I was eight!"

"Funerals are an occupation for us, darling, you're used to them. Peach . . . isn't. Uncle Edisto's funeral was Peach's first experience with death. And he's very sensitive; that's just the kind of person he is."

"*I'm* sensitive! You said so yourself when Tidings teased me about sitting in my closet."

"You're a different kind of sensitive, Comfort. You sit in your closet—you're sensitive inside. Peach cries—he's sensitive outside. That's all. We each do something to cope with our feelings when life feels overwhelming—Tidings mows grass."

I thought about that. "Mowing grass is useful! And sitting in the closet never hurt anybody! But Peach cries and carries on and makes everybody miserable!"

Mama stopped pulling the wagon. I pressed my case. "I couldn't go fishing with Uncle Edisto whenever Peach visited. His screaming scared away the fish—*'This boat's rocking too hard!'* and *'Don't hurt that worm!'* I don't know how Uncle Edisto could stand it!" I took a breath.

Mama dabbed at the perspiration on her neck and spoke in an even voice. "Uncle Edisto loved Peach."

She regarded me with a cool eye. "He had infinite patience."

I pretended to study a caterpillar in the grass at my feet.

"Uncle Edisto was the closest thing Peach ever had to a daddy," Mama said. "His death devastated Peach."

"He ruined Uncle Edisto's funeral!"

"For whom? For Uncle Edisto? If he had been able, Uncle Edisto would have worked hard to comfort Peach."

I began to feel as low as the caterpillar.

"You might give him another chance," Mama said. "The only way he will learn some decorum is by practicing."

I wanted to have the last word, but I didn't know what decorum was. I crouched back down in my wagon-pushing position. "All I can say is, we'd better have a lot of Kleenex ready."

Mama smiled. "Let's get out of this sun—I'm melting out here and so are my flowers!" We wrestled the wagon through the side door of the funeral home and made our way down the cool, quiet hallway. I knew Daddy was busy with Great-great-aunt Florentine. We passed the casket room and Mama said, "Stop." She checked on Merry. "Still sleeping."

We pulled the wagon into the cavernous downstairs kitchen, where the air-conditioning made the room so cold, I could imagine what Admiral Byrd felt like as he reached the South Pole (*Discovering Our World Magazine,* issue 17)—only he didn't have a long table full of funeral food standing ready for guests. We studied it, in a moment of silence.

"There's Mrs. Elling's chicken-and-potato-chip casserole," I said.

"Folks have been bringing food all day," said Mama. She removed her gloves and with a sigh looked around her. Great-great-aunt Florentine had always been in charge of the downstairs kitchen on funeral days and I'd been her assistant.

"You want me to help with the food?" I asked.

Mama shook her head. "Jimmie can do that just fine when she gets here." She sat down at the kitchen table and sagged a little. Mama rarely sagged. She put her elbows on the table and clasped her hands together and leaned one soft cheek on her hands and looked at me sideways. "Will you eat tonight if you don't come to the viewing?"

I brightened. "I promise."

Mama paused and then said, "You'll have to see him sooner or later, you know."

"I know. Later's better than sooner." Then I remembered. "Declaration says she'll come tomorrow, too."

Mama lifted her head and gave me a quizzical look. "Really?"

"Really. She told me so at Listening Rock just now . . ."

"Come here." Mama took two fingers and tucked wayward strands of my hair under the brim of my baseball cap. "This hair . . ." She patted my cheek.

"I'll wash it."

She cupped my chin in her hand and whispered, "How will you stay away?"

I blinked at her and shrugged.

Mama looked deep into my eyes. "Are you okay?"

My heart fluttered into my stomach. "Why?"

"You and Aunt Florentine were such a pair," said Mama, straightening up and repositioning the clip in her hair. "To lose both Florentine and Edisto in the same year . . . It's a hard blow, for heaven's sake."

I swallowed and tried to remember: *Death is a part of life.*

"It's a blow for Peach, too, you know," said Mama.

"Please don't make me play with him, Mama."

At Uncle Edisto's funeral, Peach had fainted into the punch bowl, and that was just for starters. He had been so overwrought about everything, I almost had to strangle him and put him into the casket right along with Uncle Edisto. Only my strength of character kept me from it.

"I thought you live to serve," said Mama. Her voice was tired. She put an arm around my waist and pulled me to her, leaned her head on my shoulder, and gave me a squeeze. I stood there in my half muddy, flip-flopped feet, with my hair sticking out from under my baseball cap, and clutched her right back.

"Okay," said Mama. "You're off duty tonight."

We heard Merry, awake and singing. She called from her casket, to the tune of "Jingle Bells": "Get me up! Get me up! Get me up away!"

I did.

Chapter 8

Lurleen finally came and brought Jimmie, and I escaped upstairs—above Snowberger's, above the arriving food and gentle wishes—to a long bath with bubbles and then my lookout post in Great-great-aunt Florentine's room. It was almost dusk, that magical time of evening just before the fireflies come out, just as the crickets start up their all-night racket. For years Aunt Florentine and I had sat together at her window and watched folks arrive for viewings and visitations and funerals. "Geography," said Aunt Florentine as she told me stories about how Mr. Brunner wore a toupee, how Mrs. Ragsdale had married the wrong man, how I'd better not eat anything Tot Ishee brought to a funeral.

I learned a lot of facts for my book, *A Short History of a Small Place.* I told Great-great-aunt Florentine I'd give her credit in the acknowledgments. She told me I should dedicate the book to her. Maybe I will.

So it was from my lookout post in Great-great-aunt Florentine's room that I saw Peach arrive. His mama, my aunt Goldie, pulled into the front parking lot in a long blue car with fins on the back for taillights. It looked like a spaceship. I could see Peach inside. He wasn't moving. That couldn't be good.

Aunt Goldie was out of the car as if a bumblebee had stung her—hugging Mama, hugging Daddy, hugging anybody who would let her wrap her arms around them.

People began to hover around the passenger side of Aunt Goldie's car. They peered through the glass, tapped on it, gestured to Peach inside. He didn't budge.

"Here we go," I said to myself.

I sat at the window seat and peered through Aunt Florentine's binoculars. It took three people to pry Peach out of the car. He was as stiff as a stalk of celosia, already up to his ears in overemotional shenanigans. His eyes were clamped shut, and his face was as ashen as the dead.

I saw the concern on Aunt Goldie's face, and I

watched Mama pat on her, pat on Peach, and exchange a tired look with Daddy. Daddy shook his head as people carried Peach into the house. Then he reached for Mama, just as he always did, and Mama kissed his face, just as she always did. I flopped across Aunt Florentine's bed, resigned to a weekend of misery.

I lay as still as I could, as still as dead people lie when they are in caskets, as still as Aunt Florentine was lying downstairs in the Serenity Suite, waiting for family and friends to come calling at seven o'clock sharp for her viewing.

Everything in Aunt Florentine's room sounded slow and soft. The floorboards breathed a creaky breath. The mantel clock gave off a satisfying *tock-tick, tock-tick, tock-tick* sound that made the wallpaper roses look like they might nod off to sleep. Specks of dust drifted in the sifts of dusky light that came through the window blinds. The dust had no one to land on anymore; Great-great-aunt Florentine was gone. I breathed softly in and out on the bed and felt the loneliness of everything.

I thought about the days when Great-great-aunt Florentine played old maid with me and Tidings. When Declaration spent the night, Aunt Florentine gave us egg-white facials, shared all her beauty tips, and let us rummage through her jewelry box. I stared at her bedroom door now and waited for her to come through it, with her teeth in a glass of water and her face glistening with face cream, ready for bed at five o'clock in the afternoon like always. But she didn't come in, of course.

I turned over. Even Aunt Florentine's pillows looked lonesome. I could almost hear Aunt Florentine say, *These are my pillows, which I have left for you. Enjoy them and remember me.* So I gathered them up. I tucked one under each arm and traveled across the wide hallway to my room.

I propped myself against my closet wall with the two feather pillows that smelled like lavender and that had belonged to Great-great-aunt Florentine. I missed Dismay, but he was a funeral dog, so I knew his place was downstairs at the viewing. He'd sleep next to Great-great-aunt Florentine's casket for the night—that was his way. He'd already be in the thick of everything, and folks would be patting all over him. That would make them feel better. And Dismay *loved* Peach. Peach would be sneezing. He was allergic to dogs.

It was cozy in the closet. I had an overhead lightbulb that I turned on and off with the pull of a long string. My small dresser was in the closet. My hanging clothes surrounded me like loving aunts and uncles telling old family stories. A big piece of carpet with a cabbage-roses pattern all over it lay on top of the wooden floor. All around the edges of the carpet, I put my Essential Equipment. First, a dictionary (I looked up the word *decorum*: "Good taste in conduct; dignity." *Peach* and *dignity* would never exist side by side—what was Mama thinking?). Next, stacks of *Discovering Our World Magazine.* My *Short* notebooks. An art tablet for drawing and thinking; a mayonnaise jar full of number-two pencils (recently sharpened) with good erasers; a wooden ruler (accept no substitute); a box of colored pencils; and my crayons. I had a map project to work on for school. I was drawing a map of my closet. I opened a package of Tom's peanuts and shook them carefully into my bottle of RC Cola. I sighed and took stock.

One: I felt clean and organized. I wore my old hey-diddle-diddle pajamas—cats played fiddles, dishes ran away with spoons. I'd even washed my hair and combed out all the tangles. Aunt Florentine had loved to work on my hair. "Straight as a stick, thin as a lie, and tangled as a spider's web!" she'd say. "Let me at it!" But she wouldn't see it ever again.

Two: I looked at my watch: 7:00 P.M. Tidings would be wearing his suit and standing just inside the big front doors of the funeral home. He would greet visitors, ask them to sign the guest book, and then direct them, like he was an air-traffic controller and they were taxiing airplanes, to the Serenity Suite.

Three: Daddy would have put the finishing touches on Great-great-aunt Florentine, making sure all the buttons down the front of her favorite cornflower blue dress lined up just right; that her false teeth were inside her mouth; that her hair was styled perfectly; that every wrinkle was smoothed and powdered.

As I leaned back into Great-great-aunt Florentine's pillows, I was filled to overflowing with a longing to talk with her. I wanted to see her. I wanted to hug somebody. I wanted my dog.

Organ music drifted upstairs—which meant that Mrs. Powell, Preacher Powell's wife, had arrived. Aunt Goldie would be in the resting room with Peach, trying to keep him calm and get him to sleep.

"I'll bet she gives him knockout drops," Tidings once told me.

"She should knock him out on funeral days, too," I'd said. At Great-uncle Edisto's funeral—after he had ruined the punch bowl, after he'd spewed his lunch into a potted fern (then dribbled on Declaration's shoes), and after he had smashed himself into the azaleas—Peach lay sobbing into the flowers, and of course, I was sent to extract him from the bushes since everyone else was busy with spilled punch and vomit.

I couldn't extract him from the shrubbery without pulling on him, and I didn't want to touch him. Great-great-aunt Florentine faced right up to the problem. She threw herself into the azaleas with Peach (Mama later wondered about the dents) and said, "Well, isn't this a smart move! How clever of you to think of it! It's much nicer sitting in vegetation than it is in that stuffy old house, isn't it?"

Peach gaped at Great-great-aunt Florentine while his nose dripped onto the pink blooms. Aunt Florentine pulled a Snowberger's handkerchief from the sleeve of her dress and mopped at Peach's face. "No matter what happens, Peach," she'd said, "there will always be lots of family here to love you . . . like Comfort and me!" Aunt Florentine put the handkerchief to Peach's nose, and he blew a loud honking blow. He nodded.

"And, when it is my time for the heavenly hereafter,

I want you to do something for me—will you?" Peach blinked. "Let's make a pact, Peach." Aunt Florentine had a knack for talking sense to folks. "When I go off to Glory Land . . ." Peach moaned and Aunt Florentine held him close with one arm. "You come visit me in the Serenity Suite, and I'll know you're there. I'll send you loving thoughts—you'll feel them! We'll be as close as we are right now, here in these azaleas." Aunt Florentine patted on her thigh for effect. "Think you can do that, Peach?"

Now, I knew he wouldn't even look at her casket during the funeral, but I didn't say anything. And yet, like it was a magical spell she had cast on him, Peach nodded his skinny, pointy head and said yes.

Aunt Florentine could fix anything. I could almost hear her calling me from downstairs. She would want me there!

I scrambled to my feet, hung my pajamas on a peg, pulled on my visitation dress, and slipped on my funeral shoes. I looked into the mirror on the back of my closet door. There were my knobby knees, looking just like Tidings's knobby knees, only his were bigger (and older) and one of mine was skinned. There was my crooked smile like Great-great-aunt Florentine's; my bumpy nose like Great-uncle Edisto's; my long ears like Daddy's; my rosebud chin like Mama's. I looked great. Even my hair was behaving. Aunt Florentine would be proud.

I stepped out of my closet to go pay my respects to the dead.

Chapter 9

I walked across the hall to Great-great-aunt Florentine's bedroom and peeked through her curtains to see how many folks were downstairs. The front parking lot was full. Aunt Florentine was packin' 'em in. I wished she could have seen it!

I took the curving back stairs to the downstairs kitchen, where casseroles lined the counters. Their foil tops gleamed and twinkled in the early evening light that sifted through the half-closed blinds. Mrs. Powell was playing "In the Garden." Next to "Softly and Tenderly," "In the Garden" was Great-great-aunt Florentine's favorite hymn. It was my favorite, too. It made me want to hurry, so I scooted across the kitchen and reached for the doorknob to the hallway door.

As I turned it, a fiery hot shriek split the serenity at Snowberger's, as if touching the doorknob had set off an alarm. I was struck still—I couldn't have moved if I'd wanted to.

Right on the heels of the shriek was the longest, highest wail I had ever heard. And it wasn't coming from Daddy's office or the resting room. It was coming from the front of the funeral home, from the Serenity Suite—it was coming from Great-great-aunt Florentine!

I'd heard about the dead sitting up in their caskets and even saying, "I'm thirsty!" although I'd never seen that happen. I'd heard about the dead calling for their loved ones in cemeteries late at night, but I'd never witnessed that, and I'd been in the Snapfinger Cemetery plenty of nights. But I'd never heard of the dead sitting up in the funeral home, at the viewing, in front of all the mourners, and wailing his or her fool head off! Aunt Florentine was calling me!

I flung open the door and raced down the hallway. "In the Garden" had stopped. I tried to barrel through folks who were standing in the doorway to the Serenity Suite—"Excuse me! Pardon me!"—but there were too many people trying to get into, or out of, the room.

"I've never seen anything like it!" said Miss Phoebe Tolbert.

I turned around and ran back down the hall and into Daddy's big refrigerated workroom. I didn't even turn on the lights—I knew that room by heart. My hard-soled shoes slapped the tiled floor as I raced for the secret pocket doors. Just as I got to the doors, they slid open. Daddy was on the other side, in the Serenity Suite, saying, "Give us room, folks! Please!" He was trying to move Great-great-aunt Florentine's casket-on-wheels through the pocket doors and back into his workroom. Tidings and Mr. Johnson were trying to help him. Dismay was turning in circles, trying to figure out what was going on. I whistled for him, and he came to me, wagging his tail and panting a look that said, *This is so out of order!*

The casket was open with the top of the lid facing me, so I couldn't see around it, but I didn't need to see any more. I recognized that wail. It wasn't Aunt Florentine at all—it was *Peach.* Mama and Aunt Goldie were plastered against the open side of the casket, bent toward Aunt Florentine. In a low, calm voice, Aunt Goldie was saying, "Peach, let go of Aunt Florentine, honey. You're pulling her hair all out of shape. You know how she loved her hair just so." Peach wailed again. Anger filled my throat until it was so tight I could hardly breathe. *Peach!*

"We've got it, Bunch," said Mr. Johnson to Daddy. Mama's flower arrangements tumbled into the mourners or crashed to the floor as people tried to get out of the way of the moving casket.

Daddy held out his arms to everybody in the Serenity Suite. "Forgive us, folks," he said in his funeral director's voice, speaking above the wail. "We'll cut the viewing short tonight. I know you'll understand." Dismay panted by Daddy's side, while Daddy quietly spoke to folks who shook his hand, patted on Dismay, and eyed the wailing casket that was moving away from the Serenity Suite and into the cold workroom. "Thank you for coming," Daddy said over and over. "We'll see you tomorrow at three. Thank you all."

Tidings spotted me—he didn't seem the least surprised to see me. "Get the lights, Comfort," he directed. My heart was hammering my chest. I dashed to the other end of the long room and pushed up every black switch I came to, all six of them. The workroom flooded with the bright white light of the dead. And that's when the wailing stopped. Just like that.

Daddy slapped shut the pocket doors. I stood at the head of the open casket, finally able to take a look at Aunt Florentine, but all I could see was a sniveling little sack of skin and bones named Peach Shuggars lying on top of my aunt. He was dressed in a baggy pea-green suit and had his face buried in Aunt Florentine's old neck. He was crying all over her dead body, ruining the hair and makeup job that Daddy had spent so much time on, wrinkling her cornflower blue dress, holding on to her for dear life, and gasping, between sobs, "Don't go . . . don't go . . . don't go . . ."

Chapter 10

Aunt Goldie patted on Peach as he got quieter and quieter. She kept saying, "I'm right here, Peach."

Daddy sat down on a metal chair next to a long steel table. He put his elbows on his knees and rested his head in his hands. Mr. Johnson scratched his neck and looked lost.

My hands hurt, and I realized I had curled them so tightly into fists that my fingernails were digging into my palms. I had been clenching my teeth so hard, my jaw hurt. Tidings raised an eyebrow my way.

"I don't know what possessed him," said Aunt Goldie. "He's never come to a viewing before, so of course he's never seen . . . He insisted on coming . . . Said Florentine told him to . . . This whole ordeal has been so hard for him . . ." She looked at Daddy with tears in her eyes. "I'm sorry, brother," she said. Daddy shook his head and said nothing. Mama walked to Daddy and put her arms around his shoulders. Daddy lifted his head, and we all waited to see what would happen next.

The workroom faucet dripped a hollow sound into the big stainless-steel sink. The room was brighter than bright and everything in it gleamed.

Jimmie was the first one to move. She had been holding Merry in her arms. She leaned in closer to the casket and took a long look.

"Dead!" said Merry.

"Laws, yes!" said Jimmie.

"Well, actually, no," said Daddy.

"It depends," said Tidings.

At which point Mama said, in a brisk voice, "I'm making cocoa. Goldie, can you help me?"

Aunt Goldie nodded. "You'll be all right with him now," she said to Daddy. "He's sleeping."

"He sure is out," said Tidings, looking closely at our cousin. "That stuff you gave him before he got away from you really packs a punch . . ."

"That's enough, Tidings," said Mama. Then she turned to Mr. Johnson. "Plas, will you stay and help?"

"Wouldn't have it any other way," said Mr. Johnson.

I wanted to ask him if he had put my Life Notice for Great-great-aunt Florentine in his paper, but I felt like it wasn't the time.

Mama gave my shoulder a squeeze as she walked past me with Aunt Goldie (who hadn't noticed me) and said, "Go to bed, Comfort. We're all right behind you. Tomorrow will be a long day."

"Yes, ma'am," I said. I was happy to be dismissed. I'd seen enough.

I hugged Dismay good night.

"Hug me, too," said Daddy. I flung my arms around his neck, so glad he had asked me to.

He squeezed me back. "Off you go," he said. I wanted to say something to him, but I didn't know what to say. He gave me a slow pat and stood up. Then to Mr. Johnson he said, "Okay, Plas, let's pry him out of there."

I took the back stairs up to my room and my closet. It had started raining again. I drank my warm RC with peanuts. I listened to the rain ping the tin roof. I took a number-two pencil from the mayonnaise jar and opened my notebooks. I wanted to work on a write-up about Great-great-aunt Florentine's viewing, but how could I write about that? All I could write was *I hate Peach* over and over. I made it big and black on the page. I drew lightning bolts all around the words. And I hatched a new plan. I would stay in my closet until Peach went home. I would refuse to leave. They couldn't make me leave. I would sleep there and eat there and only come out to go to the bathroom. I would not see Peach Shuggars again. Not ever again.

CHAPTER II

I woke up in my bed. I half remembered Daddy putting me there. The ether smell that surrounded him like a cloud had lulled me back to sleep.

And now, after a night of rain—sunshine. I was lying on my back with my eyes closed. My face was warm, and from under my eyelids, I could detect the reddish glow that meant bright morning sun streaming into my room. Uncle Edisto always said, "The sun serves us on a funeral day. What a good omen!"

The day of Uncle Edisto's funeral, we'd had a morning hailstorm and a broken punch bowl, so I was glad to greet the sun. I willed it to serve me. I lay there in the shimmering stillness and let myself be washed in it.

I heard Dismay's toenails *tap-tap-tap*ping down the hallway, coming my way. He would have slept next to Great-great-aunt Florentine all night, and he'd be missing me. Sure enough, the tapping stopped outside my bedroom door and a little whine started.

Before I could get up to let him in, the bedroom door swung wide. Dismay bounded across the room—*Happy-happy-happy!*—and onto my bed. The bed shook under us, and Dismay's collar jangled in a tambourine of delight.

"Down, Dismay!" I said, but I was laughing. Dismay nuzzled his cold, wet nose into my neck and slurped my cheek with his sloppy tongue.

Then I saw who had opened the door. Right behind Dismay was Peach—*Happy-happy-happy!*—standing in the doorway with his hands clasped under his chin, his eyes shining like buttered toast, his short-short hair perfectly combed, and his whole body jiggling like the canned fruit suspended in Mrs. Martin's Strawberry Jell-O Mold Dream Dessert.

"Comfort!" he called in his tinny, puny, scrawny voice. He made a tentative chicken-step into the

room. And with the same great anticipation in his voice that he'd used when he had greeted Uncle Edisto and then Aunt Florentine, he said to me: "It's *morning* and I've come to *see* you!"

I shot up in bed like a rocket. "Out! Don't you *ever* come into my room uninvited!"

For one moment there was no movement, no sound at all. Peach stepped back. He sneezed and didn't even cover his mouth. His eyes filled with tears. He breathed in several short, quick breaths. A string of snot formed at the end of his left nostril.

My stomach twitched. Peach's dam burst, and then came the torrent of tears.

You'd have thought I'd set him on fire. Dismay scampered to Peach and sat at his side, panting, like he knew he was needed for that very thing. Peach collapsed into a lump on the hallway floor. Dismay watched with calm round eyes while Peach wailed.

Chairs scraped in the upstairs kitchen, voices were raised, and footfalls ran my way. I flopped myself back onto my pillow, flipped the covers over my head, and held them bunched in my hands at my ears, which made the sheet fit tightly against my face. I was sure I looked like an Egyptian mummy (*Discovering Our*

World Magazine, issue 12), and I began to picture my-self in my pyramid, closeted away from everybody.

But there were too many people in the throne room. I could hear Mama and Aunt Goldie scooping Peach off the floor. Merry *clunk-clunk*-toddled down the hallway in what sounded like Mama's high heels.

Peach would not be silenced. His thin, piercing wails rose and fell, just like the noon whistle that sounded every day at the Snapfinger Volunteer Fire Department.

"Hush, now, sugar-darlin'," I heard Aunt Goldie soothe. "*Shhh-shhh-shhhhhh!* It's going to be all right, Peach Pie."

I rolled my eyes under my sheet-shroud.

Peach stopped wailing long enough to sneeze three times violently. I heard Merry's voice. *"Ewwww!"*

"Here, Merry," said Mama. "Wipe it off."

"Stop, Peace!" said Merry.

And finally, Peach stopped. "C-C-C-Comfort!" he gargled, through a throatful of tears.

"Let's get you some water, darlin'," said Aunt Goldie. "That's a good boy. Then you can tell me all about it."

Peach sobbed and sniffed, and I heard leaving noises, the kind of settling-down, murmuring noises that drift across people when they are all talking at once, softly, ending a conversation or starting the next one. Dismay's toenails clicked down the long hallway as he did his funeral-dog duty and trotted after the sniffling Peach. Wherever there was grief, there went Dismay.

I knew Peach would make me sound like Bloody Mary, queen of England, ordering another beheading (*Discovering Our World Magazine,* issue 222). I needed to get up and defend myself.

I felt an inquisitive *pat-pat-pat* on my arm. I turned my head and peeked out from under the sheet. There was Merry, staring at me with wonder written all over her face.

"Dead!" she said.

"No," said another voice—Mama. She pulled the sheet off my head, a long, slow pull. She wore her flowing blue housecoat with the moonflower pattern, and she had her makeup on already. She was beautiful.

"I'm sorry," I said in my most miserable voice. And I was. But I wasn't.

Mama sighed. "What happened?"

"He surprised me," I said. "I hate surprises."

"Yes," said Mama. "Well . . . We could hear you scream at him, all the way in the kitchen."

"I didn't scream at him!"

"Someone did," said Mama. "And she surely sounded like you."

Mama sat down on the end of my bed. She put a hand on my shrouded leg. Her fingernails were painted a dusty rose color, and her hands didn't look a bit like a gardener's hands. Merry took one of Mama's hands and started playing with it, patting it between her own chubby hands.

Mama said, "This is going to be a long day, Comfort. Aunt Florentine was like a mama to your daddy—she practically raised him and your aunt Goldie all by herself. Last night was difficult . . ."

I interrupted Mama. "Doesn't Peach get in trouble for *his* behavior? He can do anything he wants and never get in trouble—here he comes, into *my room* . . ." I mimicked a Peach voice. "'Comfort! It's *morning* and I've come to *see* you!'"

I was on a roll and I couldn't stop. "I'm not Uncle Edisto. I'm not Aunt Florentine. I'm not going to tell him to come see me—I want him to go *home*! I don't ever want him to come back!"

"Calm, Comfort . . ."

"I can't calm! He's horrible! He ruined everything last night! You'd have skinned me alive if I'd behaved the way he did!"

"How do you know what happened after you left, Comfort? Or, for that matter, what happened this morning before you woke up?"

"I know because Aunt Goldie never yells at Peach or makes him behave!"

"Yelling never solved anything, Comfort," said Mama. "You don't know what Aunt Goldie contends with all by herself, and it's none of your business to judge. Peach will grow up and he will grow out of this phase . . ."

"Not soon enough for Aunt Florentine's funeral!" I spit. "I'm not going to the funeral, Mama! I'm not going *anywhere* as long as Peach is here!"

Mama folded her beautiful hands in her lap. She looked at me with steady eyes and said, "Listen to me, Comfort. I know how much you loved Aunt Florentine, and I know how much she loved you. You don't want to miss this funeral." That much was true. "This is going to be a hard day for everyone, but especially it will be hard for Daddy and Aunt Goldie. Can you imagine what they must be feeling?" Mama had tears in her eyes.

My eyes felt a little teary, themselves. I shook my head.

"So," said Mama, "let's think about others today. Let's help Daddy and Aunt Goldie. I suggest we *serve*."

"How?" I wiped at my eyes with the heels of my hands.

"I want you to be a good friend to Peach today," Mama said.

"No!"

"Now, Comfort . . ."

"No!"

"Comfort!" Mama gave me her *I'm shocked at this response!* look. She let the air settle around us, and then she said, "*After* the visitation, *after* the funeral, *after* the graveside service . . . that's when I want you on duty. Play a game with him—"

"He always loses and he always cries!"

"Take him to the oak grove—"

"He doesn't like to go outside," I said morosely. "He'll sneeze and complain. *'Comfort! It's too hot!'* and *'Comfort! Bugs!'*"

"Stay inside, if you prefer. Come upstairs and make some cookies. Do something you like to do, and do it with Peach."

"What about Tidings! He never has to help with Peach!"

"Tidings is going to be helping your daddy. He's going to help where he's most needed. You are most needed right here, with Peach . . ."

"Oh, Mama!" I sat up and stretched my hands toward Mama in a plea for mercy. "Don't make me!" Mama captured both my hands in hers and squeezed them. Merry watched us with blinking eyes and an open mouth.

"Comfort." Mama closed her eyes and touched the tip of her tongue to her top lip—she always did that before she said something important. Then she began. "I know this is hard, sweetheart; I do. But you are the best person for this job. Peach adores you . . ."

"I hate him!" I began to cry.

"Sshhhh," said Mama, which made me cry more. She scooted up next to me, still holding my hands. "Peach will listen to you . . ."

"No, he won't!" I tried to tug my hands away from Mama. "He never listens to me; he just cries until he gets what he wants! He's a big baby!"

Mama held on tight and spoke in a voice full of finality. "We will get through this day."

I looked at her in silence. I wanted my hands back. She released them. Tears filled my eyes. I tried not to blink. A silent Merry studied me and Mama. She had not moved from her spot.

"What about Declaration?" I asked.

"I'll ask her to help, too," said Mama.

"She'll say no," I said. I hiccupped.

"No, she won't," said Mama. "Not if I ask her. And I will."

"I told her she wouldn't have to get *near* Peach!"

"Shhhh," said Mama. "It's already decided."

I wiped at my eyes with my fingertips. "She'll hate this," I said. *She'll hate me,* is what I wanted to say.

"Let me handle it," said Mama. "It will be all right."

"Yes, ma'am," I whispered. I'd have to find Declaration before Mama did, and tell her it wasn't my idea.

"We live to serve," said Mama, quietly and firmly. I opened my mouth, but Mama held her index finger in front of her lips in a "Shush," so I just hiccupped again. Mama's lipstick was a creamy rose color; it outlined her lips perfectly, and it matched the color of her fingernails. "You will not regret that you helped your family today." No nose-kiss to seal the deal, but I knew it was decided.

Tidings's voice drummed up the stairs, sounding as commanding as General Robert E. Lee's at Gettysburg: "It's nine o'clock! Visitation's at three! Let's move-move-move! Where are the hedge clippers, Mama?"

And then, "Comfort! Declaration's here!"

CHAPTER 12

"Declaration!" I sniffed so quickly, I nearly choked on my tears.

"My gracious, she's early!" said Mama.

"Can I go?" I asked.

Mama stood and retied the tie on her housecoat. "Go on. But you've got to apologize to your aunt Goldie and Peach. I want today to be a peaceful day, Comfort."

"Yes, ma'am," I promised, in a rush to see Declaration. I threw my arms around Mama's waist and hugged her. The smell of gardenias floated all over me, followed by Mama's arms around my shoulders, hugging me back.

"I'll do a good job today," I said, my voice muffled into Mama's middle.

"I know you will, sweetheart."

"Good job!" piped Merry. She grabbed Mama's leg and hugged it. Mama picked her up and kissed her.

I banged into Tidings as I headed into the hallway.

"Easy, Private!" Tidings said as he grabbed me. He smelled like cut grass and sweat, already, at nine in the morning.

"Front or back?" I asked. The front parking lot is for visitors; the family lot is in back.

"Front hedge," said Tidings. "That's the one that visitors will see."

"They're in the flower shop," said Mama, coming toward us.

"No, no!" I said, disentangling myself from Tidings. "Where's Declaration!"

"Don't worry about the hedge," said Mama, touching Tidings on the arm affectionately. "You just trimmed the hedge last week, darling."

"He likes power tools," I said as I stepped between them.

"I like order," said Tidings, unoffended. "The troops are reconnoitered in the back parking lot."

"Thanks!" I ran toward the back stairs.

"Shoes!" called Mama.

"Clothes!" said Tidings. "You're out of uniform, Private!"

"Later!" I called, running down the back stairs. My hey-diddle-diddle pajamas flapped after me. I almost tumbled into Daddy as I ran toward the back door. He looped a long arm around my waist and scooped me into his arms. Dismay appeared, jumped his big front paws on us, and barked.

"Where's the fire?" Daddy asked. "Down, Dismay!"

I thought of refrigerated Aunt Florentine in the next room. I longed to see her. Instead I buried my face in Daddy's neck and said, "I love you."

"Good," he said. "You've always been my girl." His whiskers tickled my face, and I could feel the vibration of his voice in his neck.

"Declaration's here!" I wriggled out of his embrace.

"I know." He opened the back door. "I'm heading her way right now. Her daddy's got some extra newspapers for me."

"My Life Notice! Did it make the paper?"

"I don't know, honey . . ."

I ran ahead of both Daddy and Dismay, and rounded the back corner of the house. Mr. Johnson waved a hand at me as he walked toward the house with an armful of newspapers. I waved back at him. "Did I make it? Did my write-up get in the paper?"

Mr. Johnson smiled a crooked smile and shook his head. "I'm sorry, Comfort. Just the facts, ma'am."

"But those *are* the facts, Mr. Johnson!"

"They are the facts according to Comfort," said Mr. Johnson. "I need birth dates, death dates, marriage dates . . . Facts, Comfort, not opinions. If everybody reported the news with an opinion, who could we believe?"

"I always believe Miss Phoebe Tolbert," I said, "and she's full of opinions!" Miss Phoebe Tolbert wrote the columns about everybody's comings and goings around the county.

"That's different," said Mr. Johnson. "That's not news. That's . . . I don't know what that is."

Dismay was at my side, wagging his tail at Mr. Johnson. The parking lot was warm under my bare feet. By afternoon it would be too hot to stand on without shoes. Mr. Johnson patted Dismay and said to me, "Keep trying—it was a good write-up . . . but not yet newspaper worthy."

What he meant, of course, was, It's not yet boring enough. I just didn't think I could be boring enough for the *Aurora County News.*

Mr. Johnson clapped his free arm around Daddy's shoulder, and I walked to Mr. Johnson's car to see what was keeping Declaration. As I got closer, my eyes stared harder, my legs slowed down, and my heart started pounding.

There, in the backseat of the car with Declaration, were two more girls from school. Kristen and Tiffany. They teased me on the playground: "Comfort sleeps with dead people in her house!" We stared at one another. Dismay circled the car and panted, willing everybody in the car to come out. Declaration tentatively opened the back car door a few inches, and my heart squeezed in on itself.

CHAPTER 13

Immediately, Dismay shoved his muzzle into the opening Declaration had made. His whole body quivered with delight—*New people! New people!* His tail paddled the late-summer air.

"Get away, dog!" squealed Kristen.

"I'll stay in the car!" cried Tiffany.

"Comfort!" yelled Declaration. "Call off your dog!"

Before I could say anything, Daddy called to Dismay and he bounded to Daddy—*Happy-happy-happy!* for any attention.

Declaration, Kristen, and Tiffany climbed out of the car and faced me. Kristen was wearing a pink shorts set. Tiffany wore a yellow shorts set. Declaration's shorts set was light blue. Gone were the dresses Declaration always wore. Gone were the gloves, the hat. She didn't look like Declaration at all! She looked like a Kristen-Tiffany-Declaration triplet in matching ankle socks and ponytails. I couldn't think of a thing to say.

"Nice pajamas," said Tiffany.

Kristen giggled.

Declaration looked at me and sighed.

I licked my lips. The silence itched like a mosquito bite.

Finally, Declaration spoke in an uneasy voice. "Jennifer's having a birthday party."

"We're going bowling!" said Tiffany in a bright voice, as if going bowling meant flying to the moon.

"Declaration's daddy is driving us!" Kristen yipped.

I loved birthday parties. "It'll only take me a minute to get dressed," I offered. I didn't even like Jennifer. I didn't have a shorts set. But if they had come all the way to Snowberger's to get me . . .

Kristen and Tiffany looked stunned.

I felt my face on fire with embarrassment. *What?*

"Comfort," said Declaration, looking at the other girls and then back at me. Kristen and Tiffany were watching Declaration, and I could tell she knew it.

"Kristen and I spent the night at Tiffany's house last night."

Kristen and Tiffany smiled at me.

Declaration continued. "Daddy picked us up for the party. We stopped by so Daddy could drop off the paper . . ."

"What time is the party?" I interrupted. "Maybe Daddy can run me over to the bowling alley if you want to go on ahead before I get dressed."

Kristen and Tiffany had entwined their arms. They studied the asphalt at their feet.

"It's at ten o'clock," said Declaration, "but, Comfort . . ."

That meant I could stay away from Peach all morning! "Of course, I'll have to ask Mama if I can go."

Tiffany put her hand over her mouth and stifled a giggle. Declaration looked at me, wide-eyed, and I stared back at her in a helpless way.

"Comfort!" said Declaration from between clenched teeth. She gave her head a tiny tight shake.

Tiffany spoke next. "Don't you have an *obituary* to write, or something?"

My heart began a wild beat in my chest; no one at school knew about my Life Notices but Declaration.

My heart was thumping so hard, I could barely breathe. I didn't know how to turn around or how to leave. I stared at the air in front of me.

Declaration was suddenly at my elbow. She stood with her back to Tiffany and Kristen. "You can't go to a party on a family funeral day, Comfort." She used one finger to touch my arm. "I'll tell you all about it later."

I blinked. Everything moved in slow motion. "Yes," I said. "I mean . . . no . . . That's right . . ."

In that moment a tinny, puny, scrawny voice called to me from the direction of the funeral home. "Commmfort!"

Time came back to me. Peach was running in my direction, waving his skinny arms in the air, his head bobbing on his thin-as-a-noodle neck as he ran. His whole body careened first right, then left; he was like a bony little bird flapping out of control.

"What is that?" said Kristen.

"What's wrong with him?" asked Tiffany.

Declaration put her hands on her hips. Peach stopped in front of her and swallowed. He tried to talk, but he was out of breath from that crazy running, so he just stood there, making great gulping sounds with fishlike lips, trying to get his breath back.

"What is he . . . slow?" asked Kristen.

"No," I said.

Tiffany giggled and said, "He sure is *neat*."

Now, Peach didn't act orderly, but he was the most orderly-*looking* person you would ever want to meet. Every single day he looked like he had just walked out of Sunday school: Every thin yellow hair on his pin-head was perfectly cut and licked to a gloss. He wore a white button-down shirt and long brown pants, with shiny brown shoes. He was scrubbed so clean, his pale skin seemed to glow.

"I'm sorry, Comfort!" said Peach in his sandpaper screech. "I'm sorry to surprise you so bad! Mama says you are grieving, too!"

"Get away, little boy!" said Kristen, waving her hand like she was shooing a fly.

"Leave him alone!" I said, surprising myself.

Declaration, who was looking past Peach, said, "Here comes Dismay!" Like a shot she was back in the car. "Get in!"

Kristen and Tiffany screamed at the sight of Dismay racing for the car, his mouth open and his tongue flopping everywhere.

Behind Dismay was Mr. Johnson, smiling and making for the car with a brisk step. "Dismay!" he called.

Dismay turned in midgallop and ran back to Mr. Johnson. Mr. Johnson stopped to rub Dismay all over. It made him smile even wider. "*You* are a feel-good dog!" he said. To me he said, "We'll see you at one, Comfort. I'm coming early to help your daddy."

"Yessir," I said.

"Yessir!" said Peach.

Mr. Johnson gave Peach a pat on his slicked-up hair and climbed into his car. I turned on my bare heel and stalked back to the house.

Peach was right behind me, flapping in his gooney-bird way and out of breath.

"Comfort!" he called. "Mama says you need a hug!"

I walked faster. I heard the big tires of Mr. Johnson's car roll over the pebbled entrance to the driveway and turn onto the road, away from us, toward town. I ran for the back door of the funeral home.

"Commmforrrt!" Peach implored. "I've come to *see* you!"

I opened the back door and faced my zigzagging cousin.

"Get lost!" I shouted. I slammed the door in his face.

I scaled the back stairs two at a time.

Chapter 14

I stayed in my closet until the noon whistle began to blow at the Snapfinger Volunteer Fire Department. Of course, Peach had wailed to high heaven when I'd slammed the back door. The sound of his boohooing followed me up the stairs and all the way to my closet.

No one called for me; no one came looking for me; and I hadn't done one thing but lie on my cabbage-roses carpet and breathe in and out for almost three hours, clutching one of Great-great-aunt Florentine's pillows. Maybe I even fell asleep once or twice.

The closet was a good place for listening, almost as good as Listening Rock. I could hear life going on at

Snowberger's while I stayed in my closet. Tidings trimmed the hedge out front. He sang "From the Halls of Montezuma" while he worked. He was a terrible singer. I heard the creaking of the tin roof heating under the sun. The telephone rang a hundred times downstairs, and I heard my mother's voice talking to folks all over the countryside. I smelled good smells coming from the upstairs kitchen.

On funeral days Mama and Daddy were always so busy. "But you've got to eat!" Great-great-aunt Florentine would say. "Otherwise you'll expire!" Great-uncle Edisto always cooked his famous corn bread and good black snap beans and corn on the cob, if it was summer. Great-great-aunt Florentine fried chicken in the deep cast-iron skillet and made sweet iced tea.

"Sweet tea is an art not easily mastered by the faint of heart," she'd say.

"I feel the same about corn bread!" Great-uncle Edisto would reply.

On a funeral day we ate dinner as the noon whistle blew. We'd sit down together and hold hands around the table, and Daddy would say (for example), "Let us be thankful for the life that was Elaine Hindman," and we'd all squeeze hands. Then he'd say, "Let us be thankful for one another." We'd squeeze hands again. Then we'd eat. Then we'd go to Elaine Hindman's funeral, all of us. I got off school for more funerals than I could shake a stick at, but I always made up my work.

The noon whistle finished its one-minute blowing. You never realized how long one minute could be until you heard that whistle go on and on. It was long enough to wash your hands and get to the table on time. I skipped hand washing, and instead I pulled on my lime green shorts and my Snowberger's baseball shirt. I scrunched my toes into my flip-flops.

There was no missing dinner on a funeral day—it just wasn't done. I'd have to see Peach, not to mention Mama, who, I knew, must be so disappointed in me for yelling at Peach twice in one morning. I wondered if I could suddenly get deathly sick, if I concentrated. No. I wasn't good at sickness. I was good at death, though. Possibly I could sink right into the floor of my closet—a disappearing death. No. I would have to show up and take my chances.

Aunt Goldie stood at the eight-burner stove in stockinged feet and wearing terry-cloth slippers, with a bibbed apron over her funeral dress. She was using a rubber spatula to scoop mashed potatoes out of a pot that Tidings held upside down over a bowl. Her hair was piled on top of her head and twisted like a cone of butterscotch custard at the Dairy Dip.

Mama was settling Merry in her high chair, and Merry spotted me first. "Fumfort!" she squeaked. She clapped her small hands.

Heads turned. Peach wouldn't look at me. I wouldn't look at Mama.

Aunt Goldie gave the spatula to Tidings, wiped her hands on a dish towel, smiled at me, and said, "Come here and let me kiss you, puddin'." Her bracelets clinked as she opened her arms wide and gathered me to her. "How did I miss seeing you last night?" She gave me a wet perfumed kiss. "We need all the extra kisses we can get today," she said. "Sit-sit-sit!"

Daddy, already sit-sit-sitting at the table, pulled out my chair and I slumped into it, relieved that Aunt Goldie didn't want to throttle me. Or maybe she did. Dismay was under the table. I slipped off my flip-flops and slid a bare foot over his black coat. He licked me on the leg.

Tidings put the potatoes on the table, arched an eyebrow at me, and sat between Peach and Mama on the other side of the table. Mama busied herself with Merry. When she and Aunt Goldie were seated, Daddy put out a hand to me on his left and to Aunt Goldie on his right. Merry was already squeezing two of my fingers tight in her tiny fist. I closed my eyes like I always did.

"Let us give thanks for the life that was . . ." Daddy's voice choked. "Florentine Snowberger."

I squeezed Daddy's hand extrahard. He squeezed mine back. Peach sniffed twice and cried a short hiccupping cry. Dismay thumped his tail from under the table. The grandfather clock ticked time away in the upstairs hallway.

Daddy took a breath. "Let us all give thanks for one another," he said.

I squeezed. Daddy didn't let go, so we all kept holding hands. Soon I opened one eye. Aunt Goldie's blue eye was looking back across the centerpiece of zinnias. I opened both eyes and looked at Daddy. A long tear snaked down his cheek.

Aunt Goldie said, "And let us love one another." Daddy still held hands. Aunt Goldie said, "And let us eat this magnificent dinner that Goldie Shuggars has made! Glory, hallelujah! I declare, she has knocked herself out!"

"Out!" said Merry. "Eat!"

"Yes," said Daddy, letting go of my hand and opening his eyes. "Eat." He kissed Aunt Goldie's fingers and let them go. "Thank you, sister. It looks . . . delicious." I had never seen Daddy cry, not even when Great-uncle Edisto died. It made *me* want to cry for Daddy's sadness, for my sadness . . . for the sadness of everything. I couldn't stand it.

"I'm sorry," I blurted. I kept my gaze on the centerpiece of zinnias.

"Sorry," said Merry. She kissed my arm.

Mama stopped helping Merry's plate with butter beans. Tidings stopped sinking his teeth into a chicken leg. The air felt charged with the expectation of what might come next. Once I had started, I couldn't stop. Sadness leaked out all over the place.

"I'm . . . I'm having . . . a hard day," I said. My tears dripped onto Great-great-aunt Florentine's white lace tablecloth. I wondered what Peach thought, watching me cry, but I couldn't help it. I felt Peach-like, but I had decorum. I didn't puddle into a heap and wail.

Daddy put one hand on the back of my neck and handed me his napkin with the other. I blew my nose. Aunt Goldie got up and poured me a glass of sweet tea from Aunt Florentine's etched-glass pitcher. I drank it all down at once.

"You need to eat something, dear heart," said Aunt Goldie. "Tidings, butter this girl a biscuit." She poured me more tea and said, "When Peach doesn't eat, his blood sugar plummets and we have to pick him up off the floor and put him to bed for hours—I'm surprised you're still upright, Comfort!"

I nodded. Tidings passed me a biscuit and, because Aunt Goldie would stare at me until I did, I took a bite. Then I looked at Mama, who gave her head the tiniest nod of approval. It was all I needed. I swallowed and said to Peach, "I've got a . . . bottle cap collection. I can show it to you after dinner, if you want."

Great-uncle Edisto had willed me his bottle cap collection and Peach knew it. "The world's most amazing and thoughtfully collected collection of bottle caps in the South!" Uncle Edisto had said. I was proud of it and took good care of it.

Peach looked at Aunt Goldie. He had been studying her every word, every move. She threw her hands to her throat and said, "Oh, you don't mean to tell me!" which made Tidings laugh. "A bottle cap collection!" she said. "As I live and breathe!"

Peach brightened. "Am I invited to your room to see it?"

I could feel my face flush red, and I stared at the biscuit in my hand. "Yes."

"Glory, hallelujah!" said Peach. "I'm coming to *see* you, Comfort!" He had a toothy grin on his face and an expectant look. I gave him a halfway smile back.

"Eat!" said Merry, banging her spoon on her plate.

"Yes," said Mama. "Eat, Comfort. Everything will be all right. We'll all help each other today." She blew Daddy a kiss.

The sun slipped behind a curtain of clouds, and it began to rain.

A recipe from:

Fantastic (and Fun) Funeral Food for Family and Friends

By Comfort and Florentine Snowberger

How to Make Sweet Iced Tea

For heaven's sake, don't use instant tea, whatever you do.

Make real tea. Sweet tea. It's the Southern Way.

Here's how:

Put two cups of water into a stainless-steel pot. Cover.

Bring water to a good, roiling boil.

When the water is boiling, remove the pot from the heat and add to it four regular-sized tea bags. Use Red Rose or Luzianne tea. Accept no substitutes.

Let the tea bags steep in the hot water for ten minutes. Not eight. Not twelve. Ten.

Get out your grandmother's beautiful etched-glass pitcher and fill it half full with water. Add one cup of sugar to this water (yes, you must measure) and stir the sugar into the water with a wooden spoon until the water looks clear again, like magic. (If your name is Comfort Snowberger, you will stir until you think your arm will fall off.)

By this time, the hot tea in the pot has finished steeping. Remove the tea bags and pour this tea from the pot into the pitcher.

Stir again. Pour this tea over glasses that have been filled to the brim with ice. Add a mint leaf from your garden to each glass. Pass a plate of lemon slices. Sip in a ladylike or gentlemanly way. Never guzzle sweet tea.

Chapter 15

Rain thrummed the tin roof while we talked and ate and shared our afternoon plans, preparing ourselves for Great-great-aunt Florentine's funeral. Some of Mama's friends would come early to help; Merry would take a nap; Tidings would show Mr. Johnson how to shake out raincoats and where to hang them.

"It'll be a soggy encampment at the graveside," said Tidings. "I'll garrison some extra umbrellas."

"You do that, son," said Daddy. "I'll depend on you."

Peach picked at the food on his plate. Every so often Aunt Goldie would pat on him while she talked.

When the last bite of dinner had been eaten, Dismay trotted downstairs to begin his duties, and everybody went back to work. Peach cleared the table. Aunt Goldie washed dishes. I dried. We worked in silence, except for Aunt Goldie humming "When the Roll Is Called up Yonder."

Peach meticulously put away the pickles, the butter, the biscuits. He did one thing at a time, slowly, deliberately, completely. Later he would want to linger over every bottle cap. He'd organize them in alphabetical order: Dr Pepper, Mr. Fizz, Orange Crush, Pep Up, Southern Swirl, Vernors. Or he'd organize by colors or dents—he would have a system. It was his way.

As the last dish was stacked, as I resigned myself to spending the next hour in my room with Peach, Aunt Goldie said, "Sit!"

Peach and I glanced at each other and obeyed. Aunt Goldie brought to the table a loaf of prune bread still warm from the oven. It was her specialty—more like cake than bread, moist and rich and sweet. Peach smiled when he saw it. Aunt Goldie sliced three thick slices onto glass plates, poured three glasses of cold milk, then sat down with a long sigh and a smile back at Peach as she shook out her napkin into her lap. Peach forked a huge bite of bread into his mouth and made *Mmmm!* noises as he chewed. I stifled the urge to say, Stop! You sound ridiculous! And you have no manners! The rain drummed on the roof and the air was filled with dampness.

"This will be my favorite part of the day, Comfort," said Aunt Goldie, sitting back in her chair. "I want you to tell me everything that happened when you found Aunt Florentine dead in the garden. I want to hear it from your lips—don't leave out a detail!"

Peach choked.

Aunt Goldie's bracelets clinked as she calmly slapped Peach on the back.

I'd had a piece of prune bread headed for my mouth when Aunt Goldie spoke. I put my fork down and scratched at my cheek. "Are you sure?" Peach looked so milky white, I thought he might evaporate.

"Absolutely." Aunt Goldie nodded her ice-cream-cone hair.

So I told her everything, from finding Aunt Florentine's head resting on the mound of marigolds, to the bees buzzing around her and Tidings running for the hearse. Aunt Goldie interrupted every other sentence with "I declare!" or "Bless my stars!" and a few "Glory, hallelujahs!"

Peach put his elbows on the table and pressed his fingers against his closed eyelids until the tips of his fingers turned white.

"And how did you feel, Comfort?" asked Aunt Goldie.

Peach groaned.

"I felt fine."

"You see, Peach?" said Aunt Goldie. "She felt fine!"

Peach shuddered.

"Well, not just fine," I said. "I was kind of . . . sad, too."

"Well, of course you were!" said Aunt Goldie. "Edisto always said that death is a sadness to us all, but there isn't a death that doesn't serve us in some way, particularly when we become so old we are ready to rest. Maybe that's why seeing Aunt Florentine lying peacefully in the garden didn't make you scream or faint or run away, Comfort . . ."

I thought about that. "She was ready for dying. She said so all the time."

Peach slid his fingers around to the sides of his face and opened his eyes.

"It's true," I said.

It was. Aunt Florentine had ordered her headstone the year she turned ninety. It was sitting in the cemetery already, just waiting for the death date to be engraved on it after she died. Every evening Aunt Florentine would kiss each one of us "good night and good-bye!" and trundle off to bed saying, "I'm bound for Glory Land!" But she'd still be here in the morning. She'd shuffle into the upstairs kitchen with the eight-burner stove and the double oven, and she'd come over to kiss me first.

"You're still here, Aunt Florentine!" I'd say, and I'd scramble her an egg and feed a biscuit to Dismay.

Aunt Florentine would sneak a piece of bacon from the paper-toweled plate on the stove and say with surprise, "My heavenly bed's not ready yet!"

So, when she finally went, I figured that some efficient angel had made Aunt Florentine's bed and it was time for her to go.

"Tell Peach about it," said Aunt Goldie, so I told Peach. He held his hands tightly against the sides of his head as I spoke, as if his head might pop off his body if he didn't keep hold of it.

"So you see, Peach Pickle," said Aunt Goldie, "Aunt Florentine in the casket last night was not really Aunt Florentine . . . She has gone to Glory Land . . ."

Immediately, Peach slapped his fingers back over his eyes and squealed, "Stop!"

"She's already gone, sugar."

Peach moaned and shook his head back and forth with a forceful sway, his fingers still glued to his eyes.

"Now be still," said Aunt Goldie, stopping Peach's head with her hands. "You're going to pop an artery and give yourself an apoplexy!" She held Peach's head still until his shoulders slumped and he was quiet, then she peeled his hands from his face.

He blinked at her with enormous blue eyes. He was pale and looked like he was 285 years old, with the grief of the whole world etched on his face. My heart felt softer toward him until I reminded myself that I hated Peach. I stared at my prune bread.

When I looked up, Aunt Goldie had leaned over and pressed her forehead to Peach's forehead. They were staring at each other, eyeball-to-blue-eyeball.

"This body is a shell of who you are," Aunt Goldie whispered. She tapped Peach's chest with two fingers. "*Here* is who you are, sweet thing. It's inside, not outside. Death can't touch that."

Peach didn't move. He didn't say a thing.

Aunt Goldie planted a firm kiss on Peach's forehead. "Let us eat this cake and be glad for it." She picked up her fork. "It's *good* to be *alive,* isn't it, Comfort?"

"Yes, ma'am." I took a bite of Aunt Goldie's prune bread. It was delicious. I told her so.

"Thank you, puddin'. I always say, there's nothing like fresh hot cake and cold milk to make a body feel better on a funeral day. Throw in a bottle cap collection, and your day is made!"

Peach cleared his throat in a great gargle. "And after that, can we play marbles?" Peach coveted my cat's-eye. I wouldn't let him have it. But . . . I'd play marbles. *I lived to serve.*

"Promise you won't cry if you lose," I said.

"I promise." He picked up his fork. Color was coming back to his cheeks.

"Get dressed first," said Aunt Goldie. "Then marbles."

Peach gave Aunt Goldie a sloppy grin. We ate cake. Rain peppered the roof. It would be a wet funeral day. I was draining my milk just as Declaration stepped into the kitchen.

Chapter 16

Mercy!" said Aunt Goldie as she spotted Declaration. "I believe we have a lost kitten in our midst!"

Declaration was wet and unhappy. She mopped at her arm with a Snowberger's handkerchief.

I stood and wiped the milk off my upper lip.

Declaration had been bowling and eating birthday cake while I'd been sleeping in my closet, avoiding everyone; while I'd been crying at the dinner table; while I'd been telling Aunt Goldie and Peach all about finding Great-great-aunt Florentine in the garden. Declaration hadn't even asked me about how Aunt Florentine died. It wasn't like her. But nothing she did seemed like Declaration anymore.

"Can we help you, darlin'?" Aunt Goldie said.

"This is my friend Declaration," I said. Declaration stayed put near the door. "You remember Declaration, Aunt Goldie . . ."

"Oh!" said Aunt Goldie. "Mercy, I remember you, Declaration. I haven't seen you in ice ages! Just look at you! You've grown into a beautiful young lady!"

Declaration's eyes softened. She even smiled. "Thank you," she said, full of good manners. "It's nice to see you again." She tucked her handkerchief into her pocket. Declaration was dressed like Declaration again. She wore her Sunday school dress, gloves, and a hat. I hoped she'd gotten all gutter balls at the party.

"Have some prune bread," said Aunt Goldie. "It's warm from the oven!"

"No, ma'am, thank you." Declaration glared at me. "I'm here to . . . *help* . . ."

I swallowed and my stomach sank.

"Is it that time already?" Aunt Goldie looked at the clock on the wall and shot out of her chair. "Oh, for heaven's sake, it is! Come on, sugar, let's get dressed, quick!"

"You're already dressed, Aunt Goldie," I said.

She removed her apron. She was dressed entirely in purple. "So I am. I plum forgot. I'm wearing plum, too." She laughed at her joke. "We'll be right back, dears. Peach has a new suit! Just you wait and see!" She hung the apron on a peg by the stove as Peach put his napkin on his plate and pushed in his chair. He kept his eyes on Declaration. She glowered at him.

"We'll get these dishes later," Aunt Goldie said. "I was having so much fun, I forgot all about the time! Tell you what—we'll just see you girls downstairs. How's that?"

I nodded, and Aunt Goldie patted my cheek and gestured a *Hurry up!* toward Peach.

"Don't forget about playing marbles, Comfort!" said Peach as he passed me.

"I won't."

Declaration stared at the ceiling.

"Marbles after the funeral, Peach Pie," Aunt Goldie said as she left the kitchen, pushing Peach in front of her. "It's raining to beat the band . . . perfect marbles weather!"

Declaration eyeballed me, and in the same tone of voice she would have used to say, *The Black Plague?,* she said, *"Marbles?"*

"Did Mama talk to you?" I took a step toward Declaration but thought better of it and stepped back.

"Oh yes!" said Declaration. "She corralled me downstairs, right in front of my daddy and yours!" She walked toward me, pulling off her gloves one finger-tug at a time.

"I'm sorry," I said, trying not to take another step backward. "I told her you wouldn't do it . . ."

Declaration's voice was full of frustration. "Well, of course I'm going to do it, Comfort! How do I say no to your mama? Or to my daddy!" She held her gloves in one hand and said, "Just because *you* get stuck with Peach shouldn't mean *I* have to be stuck with him, too!" Her face was a deep, angry red. "I cannot believe you would stoop this low! I *told* you I would not go anywhere near your loony cousin!"

I shook my head at her, "No! It wasn't like that! It wasn't even my idea!"

"I'll just bet it wasn't!" said Declaration. "I know you, Comfort Snowberger!" She crossed her arms in front of herself. She was inches away from me.

I crossed my arms back at her. "Well, I know you, too, Declaration Johnson! Who did you think you were this morning, with Kristen and Tiffany, acting all high and mighty and laughing at me? That was a terrible trick you played on me! I hate it when you're hateful!"

Declaration flailed her arms at me, her gloves flapping around her fist. "I couldn't help it that Daddy wanted to stop by here before we went on to the bowling alley! I wasn't going to get out of the car, but you came running over in your pajamas . . . What was I supposed to do? Ignore you? Sometimes you are so *thick,* Comfort! I tried to tell you that you weren't invited!"

"You told them about my Life Notices!"

"So what?" She jutted her chin at me.

"That's private!" I snapped.

"Says who?" She stood straight.

"Says me! You know that!" I choked.

"Comfort, you write about the dead! Don't you think that's just the least little bit *odd*?"

"You never thought it was odd before!"

"Well . . . it's odd!"

"Who says it's odd? *Kristen? Tiffany?*"

Declaration stuck her face so close to mine, I could see the downy hairs on her cheeks—and then she hissed: "No! They don't say it's odd! They say it's *stupid*!"

I shoved Declaration fast and hard.

She slapped me with her gloves.

I was so stunned, I couldn't move. Neither did she. We just stared, wide-eyed, at each other.

An ice age later, the grandfather clock struck 2:00. We blinked, and both of us started to breathe again. I shuddered and tried not to cry.

"I'm so sorry . . . ," Declaration whispered.

"You're not my friend," I whispered back. I cradled my slapped cheek in my hand.

"You pushed me . . . ," she said.

"You hate me," I said.

Declaration shook her head. "No, I don't," she said. She smoothed the front of her dress. "I'm just . . . I'm just . . . I don't know . . . I'm just . . ."

"You're overwrought," I said.

"Yes, that's it."

"Well, I can see that. And, you're damp. You hate to be wet."

"Yes."

There was silence.

Uncle Edisto always said, "A real friend sees past the trouble and into your heart." I was willing to do that. I needed Declaration. So I asked her, "Would it help to have dry clothes? I could lend you my last year's funeral dress."

"No." She began to pull her gloves back on. "I'm not that wet."

"Are we still friends?" I held my breath.

She shrugged. "I guess so." It made my heart cramp. Then she changed the subject. "You're not dressed."

"I know." I glanced at the kitchen clock. "Do you want to come to my room?"

She shook her head. "I'll clear off the table while you get dressed. Daddy told me to be *useful.*"

"I didn't ask Mama to make you help," I said, but she didn't comment on that.

"I'll meet you downstairs," Declaration said. She picked up my plate and glass and walked them to the kitchen sink.

I felt like a balloon that had just been popped. I listened to my flip-flops flap against my heels as I walked to my closet, where I listened to the rain falling while I got dressed.

CHAPTER 17

I felt low, going down the back stairs, until I ran into Daddy coming *up* the back stairs to get me so I could see Great-great-aunt Florentine before he opened the doors to the Serenity Suite. Aunt Goldie had had her time with Aunt Florentine early that morning, and here was my chance to say good-bye, after all. Dismay greeted me as I arrived, and I hugged him. He was wearing a wreath of lavender that Mama had woven through his collar. Mama, Daddy, Tidings, Merry, and I stood at the open casket one last time, staring at the glory that had been Great-great-aunt Florentine.

"She looks so natural, Bunch," said Mama.

Tidings poked me in the side. I poked him back.

Daddy put his arms around all of us. "It's just us now, rattling around in this big old place."

"We'll do fine," said Mama.

"Your flowers, Joy . . . ," said Daddy. "You outdid yourself."

"I think I did, at that," said Mama, delighted. Flowers were crammed into every available space behind the casket, on the casket, around the casket. The room smelled like a lavender heaven.

"There sure are lots of 'em," I said.

"It will make troop movement difficult," said Tidings.

"We'll manage," said Daddy. "There'll be plenty of room in the parlors and folks can mingle."

"You don't suppose this rain will keep folks away?" Mama moved toward the chairs with Merry in her arms.

"I think we'll have a full house," said Daddy, following her. "In fact, I think the rain is letting up."

Mama and Daddy sat down on the front row of chairs and put Merry between them. It looked so strange, because Daddy never sat during a funeral. He was always on his feet, helping . . . serving. Tidings and I were left looking at Aunt Florentine for the last time.

"She looks so . . . ," said Tidings.

"Don't say it," I said.

Tidings put his arm around my shoulders and I leaned my head on him. I'd seen people do this a thousand times, and now I knew why. It felt good.

"She was a lot of fun," said Tidings.

I nodded my head. "She said you were going to end up the Big General of the Whole Shebang."

"She was right."

I blew a kiss to Great-great-aunt Florentine. I knew she wasn't in that shell, and yet, at that moment, I felt like she kissed me back. It was all I wanted.

"It's time," said Daddy. He stood up and looked at his watch. "Are we ready?"

"Ready!" said Merry.

Daddy kissed her. "Here we go."

A magnificent spray of white carnations, red roses, lavender, and baby's breath blanketed the length of Great-great-aunt Florentine's closed casket. The Serenity Suite began to fill with our damp friends and neighbors—our Snapfinger family. Declaration stood by the doors with Mr. Johnson, being useful. I left her alone.

Folks streamed into the Serenity Suite like water

eddying around rocks, trickling their way up to the casket, swelling around to the family, shaking hands, hugging, laughing, crying, and gurgling out the doors to join other mourners in the parlors and the hallway—everyone talking in low, loving, tidelike tones.

Some folks cried. If a box of Kleenex wasn't handy, I'd give them a Snowberger's handkerchief. I tucked a handkerchief into one of the big pockets of my funeral dress, just in case I needed it later.

I had managed to forget about Peach until he made his entrance. He processed down the grand front staircase, clinging to Aunt Goldie. He was stiff and straight and white. He wore a sky blue suit and a red tie with white polka dots all over it. He stared at a space in front of him, looking at no one and nothing.

Like the Red Sea parting for Moses, the crowd at the bottom of the stairs—the same crowd that had watched Peach make a mess of Uncle Edisto's funeral—parted to make a pathway for Peach.

Mrs. Powell started playing "A Mighty Fortress Is Our God," so, like a wave closing in behind Peach, we all flowed after him, ready to celebrate the life that had been Florentine Snowberger's. Dismay stood at the doorway to the Serenity Suite, panting and letting himself be patted. Peach paused at the doorway to hug

Dismay ferociously. Then he sneezed. Dismay shook himself and wagged his tail.

I had to sit in the front row with the family (I am usually a back-row sitter; from the back row I can see best and take notes). Daddy had asked Mr. Johnson and Declaration to sit with us, too. As we got settled to the tune of "Nearer, My God, to Thee," I found myself sitting next to Declaration. I could feel anger rolling off of her and onto me. I scooted a little closer to Aunt Goldie, who sat on my left. Peach sat on the other side of Aunt Goldie. He had buried his face in her purple armpit. He began a low moan, so Aunt Goldie began humming to the organ's "Abide with Me." She nudged me with her elbow, but I didn't hum along. Mama did. Merry, who was sitting on Mama's lap, started humming "Jingle Bells."

"Shhhh," said Daddy.

Great-great-aunt Florentine lay in front of us all, waiting, it seemed to me, for us to tenderly and truly send her to Glory Land. I felt she could hear us; I was certain of it. Maybe she could even hear our thoughts. *I love you!* I thought, toward the casket. *Shut up!* I thought, toward Peach. At Uncle Edisto's funeral, Peach had sobbed so much, Aunt Goldie had to take him out of the room as he gagged on his tears.

"Dearly beloved!" said Preacher Powell in his rich, Sunday morning voice.

Everybody got still.

Uncle Edisto always said, "Every ending is a new beginning."

We began.

CHAPTER 18

"We are here to celebrate life!" Preacher Powell started. I'd heard him say this 248 times. He never glossed over sadness or tragedy, but he always said, "Life is such a gift!" Now he said, "Let us celebrate the gift that Florentine Snowberger was to her family, her community, and the world."

From Aunt Goldie's purple armpit came a loud, snot-filled snort.

"Amen!" said Homer Hindman.

"Amen!" said Merry.

"Shhh," said Daddy.

Aunt Goldie whispered into Peach's head.

Declaration seethed next to me. "What are we

supposed to *do* with him after this?" I shrugged, and she hissed, "I'm not staying in this house and playing marbles with Peach Pit all afternoon!"

"Shhhh!" whispered Mr. Johnson.

Preacher Powell was looking at us. I put my hands in my lap and paid attention. I willed Aunt Florentine to see me sitting there, missing her. I smiled at Dismay, who was now in his place beside Aunt Florentine's casket. He perked up an ear at me and panted.

Through the prayers, hymns, and stories that neighbors stood up to tell, Peach moaned every time the word *death* was used. He gave forth with a low, muffled *"Gaaaaaaaaaa!"* all through the emotional remarks Daddy made about Aunt Florentine. He sounded like the little motor that *putt-putt*ed us around Lake Jasper in Daddy's fishing boat. Daddy wiped at his eyes with a Snowberger's handkerchief and spoke over Peach and just kept going.

Then something wonderful happened. As we talked and sang Great-great-aunt Florentine to heaven, a little bit of heaven opened up and came down to us. The rain stopped, the sky cleared, and the afternoon suddenly brimmed with sunlight. A sunbeam streamed through the big glass windows of the Serenity Suite and bathed Aunt Florentine's alabaster white casket in a golden light.

"It's a sign!" whispered Aunt Goldie. "Look, Peach!"

Peach snorted his snotty self upright, took one look at Aunt Florentine's casket, whooped like he'd been pinched to death, and dove into Aunt Goldie's armpit again.

Preacher Powell had the last word. "Life without end, amen," he said, "and . . . let there be sunshine!" Folks laughed and Preacher Powell beamed because his joke had been appreciated. "The family invites you to get in your cars and take part in the procession to the cemetery now, and then to return to Snowberger's for a hearty meal, where we will fellowship, one with another." As people got to their feet, he added, "Take your galoshes! It's bound to be wet!"

Dismay trotted to me and I rubbed him all over. "Good boy!" I said. Declaration took two steps away from me and asked her daddy something I couldn't hear. He shook his head. She stalked away. As she passed me, she purposely bumped my shoulder with hers. I didn't have time to think about that, as we were soon surrounded by friends wishing us well. Some even remarked that Peach had done so well, to which Aunt Goldie replied, "Oh yes, he has come a long way, hasn't he? He's quite the brave boy! Just look at him!"

The brave boy who usually held on to Aunt Goldie

for dear life (that is, until he needed to throw up into a flower arrangement) had branched out: He was plastered to Dismay, grinning all over himself, sneezing, with one hand on Dismay's back as Dismay let himself be patted and stroked by folks and led outside into the steamy sunshine. Peach went right with Dismay, and people even smiled and patted on Peach.

Lurleen and Jimmie had brought the hearse to the side of Snowberger's, just as they always did, and the pallbearers—Daddy, Tidings, Mr. Johnson, and three more of our friends—took Great-great-aunt Florentine and her casket through the pocket doors and the refrigerated workroom and out to the long black hearse for her last car trip on earth. Folks were milling around on the big front porch, gathering their umbrellas, sidestepping puddles in the parking lot, heading for cars, getting ready to follow the hearse in a long, respectful line of cars. Tidings was in his glory in the parking lot, handing out numbers to each driver, gesturing with wide sweeps of his arms, getting everybody ready to line up.

"It'll take forever to organize this crowd," Mama murmured from the porch. Next to her Aunt Goldie nodded and wiped at her eyes with a Snowberger's handkerchief. "It's five o'clock," she said. "Florentine's favorite time of day . . ." Mama hugged her, and Aunt Goldie let herself cry, which I was afraid would make Peach cry—and then I'd be stuck in the car with two criers on the way to the graveside service, where there would be more crying.

"I want to walk to the cemetery, Mama," I said with a sudden inspiration. "Can I walk?"

"By yourself?" Mama looked around.

Declaration sat on the porch swing and pretended to ignore me. Peach was standing on the front walk with his face lifted to the sun. Now he watched me and Mama.

"Yes," I said.

Declaration stared at her shoes.

"Can I come?" asked Peach.

"What did you say, sweet pea?" Aunt Goldie touched her fingers to her pearls.

"I want to go," said Peach. "With Comfort!"

"Oh no," I said. "If you think I'm . . ."

"Comfort . . . ," warned Mama. Inside I was shouting, No! No! It's not time yet! You said *after* the graveside service! But I stayed still and kept my mouth shut.

"You were going to ride with me, Peach Pie," said

Aunt Goldie. She blew her nose but kept her eyes on Peach.

"I want to go with Comfort," said Peach.

Mama and Aunt Goldie exchanged looks.

I squeezed my eyes shut and willed Mama and Aunt Goldie to decide that this was a bad idea.

When I opened my eyes, Mama was smiling a beauty-queen smile at Peach. She hardly looked rumpled. "Do you think you'll be . . . all right, Peach?"

Peach nodded his head. "Yes'm! I want to go with *Comfort.*"

I didn't offer to take him, even though I could feel Mama's gaze on me.

"I wonder if he could just walk over with you, Comfort," whispered Aunt Goldie, her eyes teeming with fresh tears. "It would mean so much to him! I'll be right behind you at the cemetery."

I set my jaw. "Yes, ma'am," I said in my most rigid voice.

Mama nodded approvingly, and Declaration smirked from the porch swing.

"Declaration?" called Mama. "Would you like to walk with Comfort and Peach?"

There was a long silent moment when I wondered

if Declaration would dare ignore Mama. Then she bobbed off the swing so forcefully, the chain jangled. She smiled a Kristen/Tiffany smile at Mama and Aunt Goldie. "Sure!" she said brightly. She walked off the porch and past Peach. "We'll meet you there!"

I frowned at her.

Dismay dashed over to me and barked. He knew we were going somewhere without him. The lavender in his collar made him look especially beautiful.

"You can come, too, boy," I said. Dismay was officially off duty, although he always went to the graveside service.

"Good," said Mama. "Take your time . . . We'll catch up."

Dismay barked and ran in a circle.

Peach whirled around and shouted the announcement to everyone: "I'm going with *Comfort*!" Folks held up a hand or clapped for him. His eyes shone with excitement.

"Glory, hallelujah!" said Peach, smiling at me with every muscle in his bony body.

"Glory, hallelujah," I said. "Let's go."

Chapter 19

The walk to the cemetery took a hundred years. I walked between Peach and Declaration, and Dismay ran ahead of us, circling back every so often to check on our progress and hurry us along. Declaration stalked all the way while Peach darted across Rural Route 2, back and forth, shouting at all the wonders he discovered along the roadside: "A caterpillar!" and "Dandelions! Make a wish!" Peach was suddenly in love with the outdoors.

My Sunday school shoes pinched my feet, and I'd forgotten how hot my funeral dress could be on a warm afternoon. I pulled my handkerchief out of my dress pocket and wiped at my face. My neck itched.

Declaration wasn't talking and Peach did nothing but talk.

"Watch for cars, Peach!" I said, irritated, even though I knew there would be almost no traffic. It was impossible to think with all his excitement. "Stop running in the road!"

He came back to walk alongside me, where he took purposeful strides forward in his sky blue suit and polka-dot red tie. He crackled with excitement.

"Look how high that corn is!" "I have a rock collection!" "Did you know I'm allergic to dogs?" "It's hot out here!"

"For heaven's *sake*!" said Declaration.

"Ignore him," I said.

"That's easy for *you* to say!" Declaration snapped. "You're just like him! Patter-patter-patter, on and on and on, about the . . . the stupidest things!"

I looked at her and my stomach hurt. Her face was flushed.

"Tiffany was right about you!" Declaration stopped.

"What?"

"Nothing! Forget it!" Declaration stalked forward.

"Comfort!" Peach was holding a sycamore ball in his hand. "What's this?" He gestured to the ground. "Look how many there are! It's like treasure!"

Nothing could dampen his enthusiasm.

We turned off Rural Route 2 onto County Road 2435, which ran between the Snapfinger Cemetery and the oak grove.

"*Oooo,* listen to that sound!" Peach said. His shoes crunched over the pebbles on the dirt road. "It's like crunching cereal with your shoes!"

I gritted my teeth. Declaration walked faster.

"I can skip!" said Peach, bolder by the minute. He skipped like a chicken, in a jagged movement of legs and arms.

"Shut *up*!" said Declaration, but Peach didn't hear her.

"Watch out!" I said, grabbing Peach by the arm as he almost skipped into a giant puddle.

"Oh! Sorry!"

I waited for him while he stopped completely, looked at the puddle, took two side steps, and then started walking forward again. "Why did you do that?"

"It's big," he said.

"The *ocean* is big," said Declaration, standing a little ahead of us with her arms crossed. A stiff breeze tugged at the hem of her dress. A bank of clouds had moved across the sun.

"Yep," said Peach happily.

Dismay came back to us and splashed through the puddle that Peach had just missed.

"Eeeeeeeee!" said Peach, covering his face as water splashed onto his blue suit.

I mopped at Peach with my handkerchief, then stuck it into my dress pocket.

Peach looked through his fingers and there was Dismay, wagging his tail and panting at him. Peach hugged him. "I just love this dog!"

"Goodie for you," said Declaration.

I didn't know who to strangle first.

The breeze had become a wind. It blew my straight-as-a-stick hair into my face. I pushed it away as Peach cried, "I bet I could climb a tree!" The cemetery was on our left, up a little rise. Headstones dotted the green grass ahead of us.

"You've never climbed a tree in your life," I scoffed. "Besides, it's going to rain. Look at that storm coming toward us. It must be raining buckets in Louin."

"How about this tree?" challenged Declaration. She was standing beside a gnarly oak with knotholes that made it good for climbing—I'd climbed it myself many a day.

"Stop it," I said.

Peach looked uncertain, confused.

"How about a mountain?" asked Declaration. She gestured to Listening Rock, winking at us through the trees in the oak grove.

"It's not a mountain, it's a rock," I said, "and we're not climbing it." Leaves snapped in the breeze like little flags.

"Why not?" asked Declaration.

We stopped walking. Peach stood close to me. Dismay had scampered ahead, to the cemetery and on toward Great-great-aunt Florentine's grave site. He knew what came next.

"I don't want to climb a mountain," said Peach.

"Who cares what you want!" said Declaration.

I made my decision. "Declaration! Go do what you want! I don't want you here, anyway!"

Peach stared at us.

"Good!" spit Declaration. "Because I don't want to be here! I had an invitation to go to Kristen's house this afternoon, and I had to tell her I was going to another Snowberger *funeral*!"

My mouth tasted sour and my eyes stung with tears. Birds called *Rain! Rain!* from the trees, the way they do before a downpour. The wind snatched at my dress. Peach edged closer to me. He kept his eyes on Declaration and didn't utter a peep.

"Go away, Declaration," I said. The words hitched in my throat and my heart pounded in my stomach. "Go be with your *friends.*"

"With pleasure!" Declaration crowed. She had a wild look in her eyes.

"Come on," I said to Peach. I was shaking. "Let's get under Aunt Florentine's tarp and stay dry."

I stepped into the cemetery and away from my friend who was not my friend. Peach was right with me.

Declaration shouted after us, and her voice was full of fury. "Go on! Go to the *graveyard*! Where they *bury* people!"

"Ohhhh!" Peach covered his ears with his hands.

I turned to Declaration. She made her eyes into big, round moons. "Go to the *graveyard,* Peach, where they throw *dirt* over dead people and leave them there for the *worms*!"

"Eeeeeeeeeee!" squealed Peach. He ran back to the dirt road as if the cemetery grass was on fire.

"Stop, Declaration!" I followed Peach. Raindrops pattered the orange dirt.

Dismay was back, circling all three of us, panting and nervous. "See?" said Declaration. "Even Dismay doesn't want to be there!"

"That's not true," I said. "He hates storms—we're about to get rained on!"

Dismay licked one of Peach's elbows. Peach clutched Dismay's head and hugged him hard. He sneezed three times. A bubble of snot formed at his left nostril.

"It'll be fine, Peach," I said. "You've been to the cemetery before."

"Has he ever!" said Declaration. At Uncle Edisto's graveside service, Peach had screamed at the sight of the hole that was to be Uncle Edisto's grave. He had yelled, "NO-NO-NO!" so many times that Daddy had to pick him up and take him to the car and back to the house.

"Yes, let's *all* get under Aunt Florentine's tarp!" Declaration said with glee. "We can look down into her grave! That's where she'll be, Peachie—dead! Forever!"

"Eeeeeeeee!" Peach screamed.

"Let's take a look, Peach Pit!" Declaration shouted over the wind. "Come on! You don't want to get wet!"

Declaration made a grab for Peach's arm. I slapped her hand.

"What's the matter with you?" I shouted.

Peach curled himself into a ball on the dirt road and began the wail I'd heard the night before, at Great-great-aunt Florentine's viewing.

Out of the wind came a clap of thunder. Dismay yelped and ran for the oak grove.

"Come on, Peach!" Declaration laughed like a maniac as she ran up the rise and into the cemetery, toward shelter at Aunt Florentine's grave. "Run!"

CHAPTER 20

Locusts, songbirds, the wailing wind, Peach—the whole world was alive with noise and the mossy smell that came before a big rain. Thunder added to the chorus with a low, powerful roll. Dismay streaked up Purgatory Hill, his ears flat back against his head, the whites of his eyes wild and terrified.

"Come on, boy!" I slapped my thighs and whistled. Dismay ran a circle around the wailing ball that was Peach, then ran back down the hill and into the grove. I yanked on Peach's blue-suit collar, "Move!"

"Mamaaaa!" he wailed, stretching his face up to the sky.

"Get *up*! It's going to pour!" I pulled him by the collar toward the cemetery and shelter.

"Noooo! Not up there!" He wrenched himself away from me, spurted across the road, and tumbled down Purgatory Hill. I raced after him. Just as I reached him, he picked himself up and clung to a pine sapling like it was Aunt Goldie. The ground under us was so soft and wet that my feet were already soaking, right through the soles of my Sunday school shoes.

I jerked at him over and over, trying to dislodge him from the tree. "You moron! You idiot! You nincompoop!" Then I let go, which was a mistake. He ran from me, wild-eyed, into the grove, toward Listening Rock.

"Not that way!" Peach fell headlong into Snapfinger Creek which was no longer a creek—it had become a lake. He came up coughing and choking. I ran in after him. The water covered my ankles. I grabbed Peach under the armpits and pulled. "Get . . . *up*!"

A sputtering Peach stumbled to his feet. "It's cold," he sobbed.

My heart caught in my throat—the water that had covered my ankles was now to the middle of my calves. "Get out! Get out!" I screamed. Snapfinger Creek was becoming an ocean.

Peach's eyes were as round as saucers. "It's getting bigger!" he screamed.

The closest high place was Listening Rock. I pulled Peach toward it. "Hurry!"

The water swallowed our steps behind us, like it was chasing us. It was cold and muddy, full of sticks and leaves, tadpoles and crayfish . . . and a dog.

"Dismay!" I screamed. He was half walking, half paddling. His eyes were intent on me. The lavender that Mama had woven through his collar stuck up like the flowers on headstones in the cemetery, stiff and straight. "Come on, boy!" Water swelled around my knees. I grabbed hold of a skinny black-walnut tree trunk and wrapped Peach's arms around it. He wailed to high heaven.

"Shut up!" I screamed.

Peach looked at me with his face dripping water and snot. Listening Rock was close—the distance to cross was four large skips on a dry day. But water had begun a slow swirl around our legs, and I was afraid it would suck us under and bash us into the trees.

"We have to get from here to there!" I said, pointing to Listening Rock. "Now!"

The water lapped at Peach's waist, at my thighs.

Peach was utterly quiet. He blinked at me with enormous blue eyes. He wasn't going anywhere. I could see he was ready to give up, to slip away from me, from the world, right there in the grove.

But then a miracle happened. Peach looked beyond me and saw my dog. Suddenly he was alive and full of feeling.

"Come on, Dismay!" Peach yelled through his tears. The swirling water sucked Dismay around a tree and under the surface of the water. He bobbed up and paddled furiously toward us. He was almost within grabbing distance.

Peach tugged on me and screamed. "Get him, Comfort! Get him!"

"Dismay!" I reached for him.

"Don't let go of me!"

"Hang on to the tree!"

I clutched Peach's blue suit in my fist and lunged for Dismay.

"Come on, boy! Come on!" My words were lost in the wind.

I reached so powerfully that I pulled Peach's jacket off. He shrieked. The current sucked me under and slammed me into Peach and the black walnut. My shoes popped off my feet. I felt Peach's body leave the tree. I struggled to my feet, gasping for air, holding the tree with one hand and pushing my hair out of my face with the other. "Peach! Peach!"

"I got him!" Peach gurgled.

His back was against a gigantic oak tree next to the black walnut, now just two large skips from Listening Rock—we could almost touch it. He was holding Dismay to his chest . . . or Dismay was pinning Peach to the tree, I couldn't tell. The trunk of the oak was so wide, it held Peach and Dismay comfortably to its bosom and kept them momentarily from swirling downstream.

Dismay shivered and remained very still, as if he knew that to move meant being swept away. And to move meant *Peach* would be swept away, too.

"Hold on!" I yelled. The water was up to my waist; it was inching toward Peach's armpits. I made a mad plunge forward from the black walnut. For a moment I had them both. Peach and I were face-to-face like two slices of bread, with Dismay between us like the tuna fish in a sandwich. I wrapped my arms around them.

And then it was utterly, completely quiet. The

downdraft arrived, that eerie second before a big storm hits, just before the wind swoops through and brings in the hard rain. The air instantly cooled. Birds and locusts stopped singing. Dismay looked at me with the saddest dog eyes I had ever seen. We were wet-nose-to-wet-nose.

"It's okay, boy," I said. He gave my cheek a tiny lick, a kiss.

Then the roar of the rain filled my ears.

"We're moving!" screamed Peach as the current began to sweep us around the edge of the oak. I looked past Peach's shoulder and ahead of us. If we swirled around the oak tree the way Dismay had swirled earlier, we'd be bashed into the rose of Sharon bushes that sprayed the bottom of Listening Rock. We'd be tangled in them and sucked under. Unless . . .

"Grab the bushes!" I yelled as we began to slide around the wide circle of the trunk.

"I can't!" Peach clutched harder at Dismay and squeezed his eyes shut.

"Yes, you can! Grab with your arms!"

Our bodies turned with the current and Peach's back scraped along the oak. He screamed, thunder boomed, and Dismay struggled out of our arms.

Peach grabbed him by his lavender-laced collar. I grabbed Peach. And there we were, jammed together like logs on a river, between two trees.

"Dismay!" Peach screamed. His chin was barely above the water.

I had no plan. My mind wouldn't work. Dismay's eyes rolled back in their sockets—Peach was drowning him. Peach was drowning. We'd all drown soon.

"Let him go!" I shouted.

Peach clung to Dismay's collar. Water lapped at his lips.

"Let go, Peach!" I screamed.

The water reached Peach's nose. He squeezed his eyes shut.

I reached for Dismay's collar. I pried at Peach's fingers as his head went underwater.

And then I did it. I let my dog go.

Chapter 21

Immediately, Peach's head popped above the water and we began moving again.

"Dismaaaay!" Peach gurgled as my dog swirled away from us and Peach took on a mouthful of water. As Peach gagged, Dismay banged into the rose of Sharon bushes and yelped, then bounced into the current and was swept away, tumbling under the water.

Peach and I were right behind Dismay. I grabbed Peach by his polka-dot tie and held on as we swung around in the current, banging into trees and each other—screaming like we were part of a carnival ride—all the way to the other side of the big oak tree where we slammed into the rose of Sharon bushes, water splashing over our heads, the current pulling us away, away.

"Grab on!" I yelled. Peach grabbed the bushes for all he was worth and began to choke. Then I realized I was the one choking him—I was holding on to his tie so tightly—so I let go. We held the rose of Sharon branches in our open arms, held them close to our chests while the cold black water swirled all around us, trying to tug us back into the current.

Peach cried a small-boy cry.

I wanted to cry, too. "Just hold on, Peach!" I shouted. "Hold on. Don't let go."

"Dismay . . . ," he cried.

"We've got to get up and out of this water!" I shouted. "Can you climb yourself inside these bushes?"

"No!" yelled Peach.

"Try!" I shouted.

The branches were slick with rain, but they were sturdy and had knobby, flowered handholds. The current sucked at me as I climbed inside the branches, working my way in little by little. The branches scraped and poked my feet through my socks, but I made myself keep on. As I worked my body into the bushes, I pulled Peach after me. He helped. I was worried about both of us falling down inside the branches and into the water just below us, but the roses of Sharon held us up, and soon I found that if I reached my hand through the bushes, I could touch Listening Rock on the other side. So I kept working my way through until I was up against Listening Rock. I pressed my cheek to its wet, solid surface. Oh, how friendly it felt!

I found a place low and level enough to slide onto out of the bushes. "I'll go first," I said to Peach.

He nodded. His face was a crisscross of scratches, but he didn't complain.

"It's real slippery," I told Peach once I had worked my way onto Listening Rock. "Just come slow."

He followed me, slipping and sliding and trying over and over again. I wrapped one leg around a skinny scrub pine in front of me. It scraped the skin from the back of my knee as I hung on to Peach and pulled him up. We grunted, concentrated, and struggled together. The rain lessened. The sky lightened. And there we were, two explorers on Listening Rock in the aftermath of a terrible adventure.

Peach's teeth clattered together and his lips were blue.

"Sit here," I said to him, motioning next to me. My Sunday school dress was torn in three places, and Peach's white shirt and blue suit pants were brown, heavy and sticky with mud. He sat close to me. We were silent. Birds began to call again as the rain moved away from us. A sliver of sun broke through the clouds and painted the woods with a deep, golden glow.

"Where is everybody?" said Peach in a dazed voice.

"I don't know." I shivered.

"Why don't they come get us?"

"Maybe they can't get here. This water . . ."

"Where did it come from?"

"I don't know."

"Is Snowberger's underwater?"

"I don't know! Be quiet, Peach. I can't think."

"Dismay," said Peach, as if he were reading my thoughts. He started to cry.

"Hush," I said, my voice cracking. "That won't help."

"He got sucked in," said Peach through his tears.

"Stop!"

"We could have got sucked in."

"We didn't! Now stop."

Peach stopped.

The flooding had stopped, too. The water was no longer rising.

Peach slipped an arm under my arm and held my hand. I let him. It felt good to have a hand to hold, even if it belonged to Peach. My mind was fixed on Dismay—my dog. Where was he? I sent him my strongest thoughts. *Be safe! Swim!*

"Comfort?" Peach was practically plastered to me.

"What?"

"I'm scared."

I let go of his hand and put my arm around his shoulders. "They'll come get us." I didn't know if they would or not.

"Comfort?"

"What?"

"You saved my whole life," said Peach.

"No, I didn't."

"I think you did."

"If anybody saved you, it was Dismay."

"It was?"

"Yes."

"I let him go," said Peach, quietly.

I shivered and fought back tears. "Dismay is a good swimmer," I said.

"Where do you think he is, Comfort?"

"Be quiet, Peach."

He sniffed. "When I . . . when I die, Comfort, will you come to my funeral?"

I let go of Peach's shoulders and mopped wet hair away from my face. "What kind of a question is that, Peach? Look—we're on this rock! We can go even higher if we need to. You're not about to die."

"I *will* die one day," he said.

I looked him in the face, that old face again. He looked so solemn.

"I just will," he said. "*Today* I almost died!" This remark set him to coughing so long and hard, I thought he might vomit, but he didn't. He carefully wiped at his running nose with his wet polka-dot tie. His eyes were full of tears.

"Here." I fished into my pocket for my handkerchief, but my pocket was a mass of mud. "Never mind."

He asked me again, "When I die, will you come to my funeral?"

"You're exasperating! Yes, yes, if you die before me—and you won't—I will come. I will be there with bells on."

"I don't want you to wear bells, Comfort. I just want you to come."

"It's an expression, Peach. It means I'll be glad to come." I thought about it. "Maybe *glad* isn't the word. *Honored* is the word that Daddy uses."

"I'll be *honored* to have you there," Peach said.

I didn't know what to say to that, so I said nothing.

"And . . . if you die before me," said Peach in a thoughtful voice, "can I have your bottle cap collection that Uncle Edisto willed to you?"

"For heaven's sake, Peach!"

"Well, if you want to will it to someone else . . ."

"You can have it," I said as fast and finally as I could.

"Thank you, Comfort. I am going to will to you my camera. It is very precious to me. Uncle Edisto willed it to me."

I looked at Peach's earnest face. "Thank you, Peach."

We heard the low *putt-putt* of a motor. I knew that sound. It was the motor Daddy put on the back of our flat-bottom boat when we fished on Lake Jasper. Peach and I both began shouting as Daddy and Mr. Johnson appeared in the boat, dodging trees and debris and calling for us.

"Over here!" I shouted, waving my arms.

"Over here!" shouted Peach.

"Ahoy!" yelled Daddy. "We got 'em!" The sound of great relief was in his voice.

I was never so glad to see anybody in my life—I hadn't realized how tired I was until that moment. Every bone in my body was cold. Every muscle throbbed.

Daddy idled the motor and Mr. Johnson looped a long rope around some branches on the rose of Sharon bushes so the boat would stay put while Daddy reached for Peach. "Are you two in one piece?" Daddy asked.

"Yessir," Peach answered for both of us. "Is Snow-berger's underwater?"

"No, son, just the oak grove's underwater. We've got us some flooding." Daddy handed off Peach to Mr. Johnson.

"It's a flood!" said Peach, as if he were saying *It's Christmas!* Then he said, "We thought you'd never find us! We've been out here for hours!"

"You've been gone less than an hour," said Daddy evenly. "It's just now six o'clock."

Daddy reached for me, and I came into his long arms, ready to hug him forever. He squeezed me to him and kissed my forehead.

Mr. Johnson wrapped a blanket around the shiver-ing Peach. "Declaration told us where to find you."

"Declaration," said Peach, looking at his hands.

My stomach clenched.

"She was on high ground," said Mr. Johnson, "but we couldn't get a car down the county road, so we had to go through Homer Hindman's cornfield on Old

Johnny Mercer's backhoe to get her. It's a soggy mess up there." He made room for me to sit next to him and wrapped a blanket around me, too. The warmth soothed me.

"Comfort and me almost died!" Peach's eyes were shining with the newfound surety of his survival.

"You're far from dead." Daddy spoke in his best funeral director voice.

"Comfort saved my life . . ." Peach's energy was fading. "Tell them, Comfort . . ." His eyes were taking on that exhausted faraway look he'd had when he was clinging to the black walnut tree.

"Rescue first," said Daddy. "This water is receding, and I want the boat out of the grove before the water is gone." Mr. Johnson retrieved the rope. Daddy reached for the handle on the motor, to steer it away from Listening Rock. He gave it a twist and the engine sputtered to life.

I hadn't said a word since we were rescued. I needed to say something, but I didn't know where to begin. I grabbed Daddy's arm and he looked into my eyes. "Daddy . . ." I couldn't go on.

"Comfort?" Daddy stopped what he was doing to look at me.

I blinked at him and tried to speak.

He put his big hand over my smaller one and looked me in the eye. "Honey?"

"Dismay . . . ," I said, and I burst into tears.

Daddy folded his arms around me and I wept into his chest.

CHAPTER 22

The oak grove was a quickly receding lake.

Daddy steered the boat around trees to the corner of County Road 2435 and Rural Route 2, where there was no Purgatory Hill and we could get up and out of the grove easily. The water was so low by the time we got to the edge of the road that we hardly needed the boat. Tidings and Old Johnny Mercer were on the road with the pickup truck and the boat trailer.

"Is Dismay at the house?" I called to Tidings as soon as I thought he could hear me.

"Wasn't he with you?" Tidings called back.

That made me cry again.

Daddy patted my shoulder. "He'll show up."

Old Johnny Mercer lifted me out of the boat like he was lifting me out of a grave. "Glad to see you, little lady." He handed me off to Tidings, who said, "You're all wet, Private." I hugged him fiercely. He hugged me back. We went home.

We burst through the tall front doors of Snowberger's into too much noise and too many people coming and going, all talking at once.

Declaration stood by the doors to the Serenity Suite, wrapped in a blanket with Miss Phoebe Tolbert's arm around her. Her hair was sopping wet. She watched me come through the front doors in Daddy's arms. I gave her my best *Go away!* look. She buried her face in her hands.

Mr. Johnson carried Peach, who had his eyes closed and his head tucked under Mr. Johnson's neck. Aunt Goldie hurried toward them. Mama burst into tears when she saw us. She didn't look like a beauty queen at all—she looked worn out. She took me from Daddy and carried me, herself, to the resting room.

Mr. Johnson put Peach in one bed and Mama put me in the other. Merry toddled in behind Mama. She was wearing her funeral dress and a lot of Mama's makeup. She wedged herself between the bed and the wall and took my hand in both of hers. "Fumfort . . . ," she whispered.

"I'll be back," said Mr. Johnson. "Let me get Declaration . . ."

"No!" I shouted.

Doc MacRee covered me and my muddy wet dress with blankets. Merry let go of my hand and stared.

"Comfort!" said Mama.

"Nooo!" I tried to sit up, but Doc MacRee held my shoulders and helped me back down. I started to cry.

Mr. Johnson touched the blankets where they covered my toes at the bottom of the bed. "I know she wants to see you . . ."

My stomach rolled over and I felt sick. "No!" It seemed to be all I could say.

Mr. Johnson walked to the door of the resting room. "I'll take her home," he said to Daddy. "I've called her grandmother and she's coming." Then to me he said, "You can see her when you feel better, Comfort."

I cried and shook my head. Daddy said something to Mr. Johnson that I couldn't hear, and they left the room.

"Dismay." I sobbed as I lay on the pillow, my hair a mass of mud and silt. I held the sides of my face with my hands. My head hurt. "We have to look for Dismay."

"We will, darling." Mama stroked my head. "We will. I promise."

When Peach and I were warmed up, Mama and Aunt Goldie helped us peel off our grimy wet clothes until we were in our underwear and T-shirts. They toweled us off. Peach was like a silent wet noodle the whole time. My thoughts skipped from Dismay to Declaration to Dismay again. Everything in the world felt wrong.

Mama held my hand while Doc MacRee cleaned my leg where the tree had ripped it up, and I cried. Peach's back was a mess where the tree had scraped it. He hardly moved when Doc MacRee doctored it. Aunt Goldie sat on Peach's bed and stroked his forehead when Doc MacRee was finished. She stared intently into Peach's face.

"He's in shock," said Doc MacRee. "Keep him warm and still." He stuck thermometers in our mouths. "Nothing's broken," he said as he finished. "I'm surprised."

Peach was white and silent.

"Dead . . . ," whispered Merry, now at Peach's bedside.

"No," said Mama, gathering Merry to her. "Very

much alive. Let's get something warm into them, Goldie. They're still shivering."

Aunt Goldie stood. "I'll make cocoa while I'm waiting to have a nervous breakdown." Peach opened his enormous blue eyes and stared at Aunt Goldie. She sat down again on Peach's bed.

Peach was silent, but I had plenty to say. "We have to look for Dismay now!" I tried to sit up. The room got spinny and my head throbbed behind my eyes.

"Not so fast," said Doc MacRee. To Mama he said, "Make her rest, Joy. She needs warmth and rest." Mama promised to do her best.

"I'm going out to look for my dog!"

"It's dark soon," said Mama, handing Merry to Daddy as he came into the room with Tidings. She pushed me gently back to the pillow. "And you're not well enough yet . . ."

"Folks are heading home," said Tidings. "They'll help us look for Dismay tomorrow."

"Dismay's hurt!" I told them. "If he wasn't hurt, he'd be here! We can't waste time!"

"First thing in the morning," said Daddy. "Dismay can take care of himself. He's a big boy. He's a strong swimmer, too."

"We won't be able to see pea turkey out there tonight," said Aunt Goldie.

"I'll go with you in the morning," said Tidings.

"We'll all go," said Daddy.

"I'll go," whispered Peach.

Aunt Goldie and Daddy exchanged a look.

"That would be fine, son," said Daddy. "Tomorrow it is. We're all worn out. The important thing is that we're safe."

"Dismay's not safe!" I cried. "You don't understand . . ."

"I understand," whispered Peach from his pillow.

It got so quiet, I could hear the crickets outside, beginning their nighttime song.

Tears spilled out of the corners of Peach's eyes and slid into his ears. "I let him go," he said.

Aunt Goldie looked anxiously at Doc MacRee and back to Peach. "What happened, honey?" she asked Peach in a tender voice.

"I let him go," Peach repeated, his voice gathering a hard edge to it, like he was a murderer and was admitting to the crime of the century.

A mockingbird sang outside the window. And then, slowly, the way a great lamentation begins, Peach started to cry—a real cry that sounded like it came from somewhere deep inside. Aunt Goldie surrounded Peach and his blankets with her whole body and held him while he cried.

"He'll be all right now," said Doc MacRee.

Daddy looked at me. "What happened, Comfort?"

How could I tell them what I had done? I covered my face with my hands and sobbed. Merry started crying from her place in Daddy's arms.

Doc MacRee spoke in kindly doctor tones. "These children have been traumatized, Bunch. They can barely tell us what happened yet. They need warm baths and clean beds and someone to stay with them through the night—many nights, maybe."

I wiped at my eyes. Mama kissed Daddy on his bearded cheek. "You and Plas came to the rescue, Bunch." She kissed Tidings, too, who was standing at the foot of my bed looking at me with tears in his eyes. "You, too, Tidings," Mama said, making him look her in the eye. "Would you help us turn off the lights, sweetheart? I believe everyone has finally gone home."

Daddy carried me upstairs, and Aunt Goldie came right behind him with Peach. The big old house got quiet, but my mind would not stop shouting. I was bigger than Peach, stronger. If I had grabbed Dismay myself—if I had just hung on—Dismay would be here right now. I could have figured out how to save us. Maybe we'd have floated away together, but we'd be together . . . somewhere. Maybe we'd be upstairs right now, in my closet, me wrapped in a blanket and drinking cocoa, Dismay sitting across from me with his big dog mouth panting, so glad to be alive.

So glad to be alive.

Chapter 23

Mama put me in a warm tub of water in her big bathroom and gently washed me all over. She told me story after story of dogs that came home; even her old dog, Rex, had come home missing half an ear and three toenails. My heart calmed as I listened to her.

"They always come home," Mama said as she shampooed my hair for the fourth time. The bathroom was steamy and felt wonderful. "Dogs have a nose for home. You won't know where to look for him in the dark, Comfort, but he'll know how to stay safe. He'll be back in the morning; you wait and see."

I wanted to believe her. I willed her words to be true.

It took three full bathtubs and a whole bar of soap to get me clean. At first the water stung my scrapes, especially behind my knee, but then it felt good. There was so much mud and so many twigs in my hair, Mama said, "Oh, if Aunt Florentine could only see this!" That made us both laugh. I thought of Aunt Florentine lying downstairs in the refrigerated room. I longed to tell her all about this day. I could have told her everything so easily, and she would have known what to do. I'd have told her all about it—and then I'd have written it up in my *Short* notebooks. What history *that* would be.

When I finally got out of the tub for good, it was black. Mama put Band-Aids on all my scrapes. She clipped my fingernails smooth where they had broken every which way while I was grabbing at bushes and trees and Listening Rock. She never asked me once about Declaration—she didn't even mention Declaration—and I sent her my best *Thank you* thoughts. She tried to get me to eat some supper, but I wasn't hungry.

Aunt Goldie was doing the same things for Peach in another big bathroom, and we never heard a peep from him.

Mama turned on my soft-light lamp and put me in

my bed. I was wearing my hey-diddle-diddle pajamas; I was sipping cocoa with extra marshmallows; and I was listening to the night sounds that were beginning all around me when Peach appeared in the doorway with Aunt Goldie. His hair was perfectly combed once again, and his pajamas had creases down the front because Aunt Goldie always ironed them.

Peach and I looked at each other and all our Band-Aids. We had survived something terrible—an unexpected, surprise flood that we had found ourselves in the middle of together. What do you say after that?

Peach lifted a hand as if to wave at me, then dropped it to his side. I lifted a hand back.

"I'm going to bed now, Comfort, even though it is very early," said Peach. He didn't come into my room and I didn't invite him in.

"Me, too."

"Good night, Comfort."

"Good night." It felt like so very little to say, but there were no more words. That was all we had.

Aunt Goldie kissed me gently on my forehead and said, "You are a hero, Comfort."

My eyes filled with tears. "No, I'm not."

Aunt Goldie sat at the end of my bed. "Yes, you

are," she said. "Peach told me what you did, and I am going to make you a hero's breakfast—a hero's breakfast for both of you!" Her eyes were calm and steady and smiling at me.

I nodded.

Mama slept with me in my bed. Merry slipped in, too. Mama hummed "Little Black Cat," my favorite lullaby, over and over, and I finally fell asleep. Then I dreamed. Declaration taunted Peach: *"Where they throw* dirt *over dead people and leave them there for the* worms*!"* She turned to sneer at me: *"It's stupid!"* Peach screamed: *"Not up there!"* Water was everywhere, swirling, freezing, black, and there was Dismay, paddling for me, paddling for his life, depending on me, asking me to help him.

I woke up with my heart pounding hard in my chest. I saw Dismay's sad eyes looking into mine, and I couldn't stay where I was. I climbed my sore body out of bed without disturbing Mama or Merry, and I tiptoed downstairs with a flashlight. Tidings was sleeping in a sleeping bag by the front doors.

"Oh, thank you, Tidings!" I whispered.

I opened one of the big front doors and stared out into the night. The sky was clear. A canopy of stars twinkled above Snowberger's. A brilliant moon hung high in the sky, a moon that could light my dog's way home. I shined the flashlight into the darkness, and I whispered for Dismay. I whistled. I took two steps onto the front porch, two steps toward the porch stairs. Maybe I could go as far as the front parking lot and he would be there!

"Comfort," said a voice I knew. I whirled around. Daddy was sitting in a rocker, all by himself in the dark. I smelled his etherlike smell. I heard the tiredness in his voice.

"Have you seen him, Daddy? Have you seen Dismay?"

"No, honey. I haven't seen him. What are you doing up?"

"I had bad dreams. I can't sleep. I want to go look for Dismay now, Daddy. I brought my flashlight."

"It'll be morning soon," said Daddy. "Why don't you wait right here with me until we can see? Then we'll go together."

Daddy opened his arms to me and I climbed into his lap like I was a baby again. He rocked and I didn't cry anymore. I breathed in and out with Daddy's breath, in the dark, waiting for my dog to come home.

I felt the ache of every muscle in my body, and as I closed my eyes, I felt the swirl of the sea around me. I fell asleep hearing the *swoosh* of the wind through the trees, the pounding of the rain all around me, and my own voice: *"Let him go!"* And I saw, in every tiny motion, my fingers uncurl Peach's fingers. I saw myself release Dismay to the black water.

Special Edition, September 6

The Aurora County News

Sizzles from Snapfinger

By Phoebe "Scoop" Tolbert

Not since Noah built the Ark have citizens of Aurora County seen such water! Galoshes and clear plastic rain bonnets have been bestsellers at Miss Mattie's mercantile in Halleluia all month. We have received—already, in the first six days of September—five inches of rain! (Normal rainfall for September is 2.67 inches. Normal temperature is 74 degrees. Normal dinner is pot roast and potatoes, but I digress.)

Storms brought disaster yesterday when the saturated ground in Aurora County began to resemble a lake in low-lying places. At the Pound o' Rest Trailer Heaven in Full Moon, plastic pink flamingos were seen floating off toward Pascagoula. In Snapfinger the oak grove became a troubled tributary of the Pearl River! Upon being interviewed for this story,

Old Johnny Mercer said, "Noah, schmoa! This grove flooded when I was a boy of eight—I remember it well!"

Well, Old Johnny must have been born in Biblical Times, as no one else remembers such water in Snapfinger before. But the BIG news is about Comfort Snowberger and her cousin Peach Shuggars, who were CAUGHT in the great water—stranded!—with Dismay Snowberger, Funeral Dog Extraordinaire, whose shaggy, comforting presence is familiar to all residents of Aurora County who have attended funerals at Snowberger's (which is everyone).

These intrepid youngsters were rescued late yesterday afternoon by Bunch Snowberger and Plas Johnson (yes, Our Esteemed Publisher). The two children are shaken but recovering, on the heels of Florentine Snowberger's abridged funeral service (interment to be rescheduled). Dismay remains missing. Sob! A search party is being organized. Stay tuned to this column for a complete write-up as events develop.

Chapter 24

Aunt Goldie's idea of a hero's breakfast was hot-fudge sundaes. She served them on Snowberger's wide front porch at 5:00 A.M. We all showed up, even Peach, who was sneezing every few seconds. He wore a square Band-Aid on his left cheek. His nose was runny and he kept a Snowberger's handkerchief in his front pocket. "I have caught a cold," he told me.

"I'm not surprised," I said. I didn't feel so well, myself.

Merry patted on him and said "Bess you!" a lot.

Daddy went upstairs to get ready for our search, and Tidings ate two whole sundaes while Daddy was gone.

I had awakened to Daddy's snoring, just as light was coming into the sky and the stars were winking out. I slipped out of Daddy's arms and checked all of Dismay's usual sleeping places, just to make sure he hadn't found his way home somehow and gone to sleep not wanting to disturb us. I tripped over Tidings as I came in the front doors, and he barely budged. Tidings would make a terrible soldier on watch. I didn't see how he would ever be a general.

It wasn't right that Dismay wasn't in the house saying good morning to everybody and begging for a biscuit hot from the oven. Nothing felt right, but I was determined to fix that. I'd had a little sleep and felt on fire to make a plan that would fix everything. In my closet I pulled on my lime green shorts and looked at myself in the mirror. My eyes were puffy and my Band-Aids made a patchwork pattern on my legs and arms. I tried to put on my Snowberger's baseball cap, but I had a knot on the side of my head that was the size of a walnut and tender to the touch, so I left my cap on its peg. Part of me wanted to stay in my closet all day with my notebooks, pencils, and Aunt Florentine's pillows; it felt safe there and comfortable. . . . I ached everywhere, even behind my eyes. I scrunched my toes into my black flip-flops, and I willed this day to serve me, to have a grand purpose—to bring my dog home.

Downstairs at our hero's breakfast, I didn't think I could eat anything, but ice cream felt good going down my throat, and so I ate and ate. "It's good," I told Aunt Goldie as she sprinkled walnuts on top of my whipped cream. I smiled a real smile at her.

Peach didn't eat. "Too stuffy," he said.

Aunt Goldie wanted the whole story. "Eat and tell your story," she said. "You need some strength before you go out looking for Dismay. It's not full light yet!"

My stomach began to feel queasy around all that hot fudge as I got ready to tell the story. I could practically hear Tidings: "You let him go? A soldier does not abandon his charge!" But I had to tell the truth about it—Uncle Edisto always said, "The truth shines like a searchlight in the midst of the fog."

My head was one big foggy swamp. My heart fluttered like a fan. I shuddered and tried taking in a deep breath. Mama and Merry sat on the porch swing, and Mama creaked it back and forth. Daddy came back downstairs, buttoning a clean shirt.

“Start from the beginning,” said Aunt Goldie. “What happened first?”

“I’ll start,” said Peach, and he began. “I was scared, so I ran down Purgatory Hill and into the oak grove.”

My head throbbed and my throat felt thick with chocolate sauce and exhaustion. I was suddenly fretful. “Wait! Tell them why you were scared, Peach!”

My mind raced, but Peach took his time answering. He had a cogitating look on his face. “I get scared of what I don’t know,” he said slowly. “And I didn’t know death. So it scared me.” Peach blew his nose. “But now I know it. Now I’m not so scared.”

Aunt Goldie dropped her ice-cream spoon onto the porch planks.

I stared at Peach as if he were from outer space.

A Carolina wren called from the magnolia trees, and full light came into the day.

“This body is just a shell of who I am,” Peach said in a still, small voice. “Death can’t touch what’s inside.” He looked at Aunt Goldie. “Aunt Florentine isn’t here. She’s somewhere else. Uncle Edisto isn’t in the Snapfinger Cemetery. He’s somewhere else. And it’s a good place.”

Nobody moved.

Peach was wearing his perfectly pleated pants and a white button-down shirt. Every hair was in place. He was exactly the same Peach as always, too shiny and bony and scrawny-necked, but he wasn't the same Peach at all.

"I would like to go look for Dismay," he said. He looked at all of us anxiously. "I let him go and he swirled away." Then Peach cried.

Aunt Goldie popped from her seat and hugged him. Daddy rubbed his face with his hands, and Mama said, "It's not your fault, Peach."

"Certainly not," said Aunt Goldie.

I knew that, too. It was my turn to tell them the truth. "It's Declaration's fault!" I spurted. "It's all her fault! Tell them, Peach!"

Everyone looked at me. Peach shook his head.

"Tell what, Comfort?" asked Mama.

My face felt hot—even my eyes were hot. "Declaration!" I said. "She . . . she . . ." My stomach lurched. My head felt like it would split open. The sun spilled up and over the pines near the Snapfinger Cemetery, and the porch was suddenly flooded with sunlight. It dazzled my eyes and made me dizzy. "She—" The ice cream I'd eaten was making its way up from my stomach and into my throat. Suddenly, Daddy was next to me, helping me hold my head over the porch railing. Up came my hero's breakfast, all over the azaleas.

"She's burning up, Joy," said Daddy.

"Let's get her to bed," said Mama.

"Dismay," I said, but the world was a blur. I was sick, very sick. The day hadn't served me. No one knew the truth but me. And my dog was still missing.

September 7

Private Snowberger:

I am issuing a regiment-wide report on The Search as of 6:00 a.m. today, Monday. Today's search in the oak grove came up with the following items:

1 garbage can
3 tires
a snakeskin
part of Homer Hindman's fence

The search team consisted of the Snowberger Squadron, the Coffee Club at Matthew's Cafeteria, and Boy Scout Troop 685, along with various friends and neighbors. No trace of Dismay Snowberger was found. It was a challenging engagement—wet, hot, buggy, and fraught with fear for what might lie under each bush or beside each rock. We persevered. Every soldier can be proud of the work we did today.

Our medic recommends complete bed rest for you, Private. The Snowberger Squadron is doing everything possible to find Dismay. We will continue to do our best daily with the available troops.

Respectfully submitted,
General Tidings Snowberger

September 7

Dear Comfort,

I am writing you this note to say I'm sorry for many things. I am sorry that Dismay is missing. I am sorry that you were trapped in the oak grove in the water with Peach. I am sorry that I lost my temper on the road—I don't know what came over me. I am sorry that you are so sick. And mostly I am sorry that I hurt your feelings.

Grandmother Lucy arrived from Mobile yesterday. She says that a lady always takes responsibility for her behavior. (She also says that real ladies do not bowl.)

She said I should write you a letter. I don't know how to talk to you right now, and I want you to forgive me. I feel like I'm four years old again—isn't that strange?

Grandmother Lucy says that I am a lot like my mother. She says that's a good thing. I hope so.

I hope you will speak to me when you see me again. I am sorry—so, so sorry. Please forgive me. Say we are friends.

Still your friend forever,
Declaration

September 7
Written at 5:45pm
from my sickbed
(thanks to you)

Declaration:

No.

Your friend for NEVER,

Comfort

Chapter 25

My room was dark and quiet. I had a cup with a straw in it by my bed. Mama gave me medicine that tasted like burned brussels sprouts. I slept for three days.

While I got better, and while my family searched for Dismay, the sun beamed all day every day. The earth dried up. You would never have known that we'd had floodwater in the countryside of Snapfinger, Mississippi.

Mail piled up on the table next to my bed. Every day Tidings would come to my room and either leave me a note or—if I was awake enough to listen—tell me about the search. Mama made him go to school, but still he searched on the way there and back. On Tuesday he said, "I even sneaked out in the pickup truck this afternoon, so I could drive to Raleigh and look."

"Did you see anything at all, any sign?" I whispered, so impressed that Tidings would risk so much for Dismay.

He shook his head. I cried. I cried a lot when I was awake. I acted Peach-like, boohooing down the front of my pajamas, and I didn't have much decorum. The least little remembrance made me cry. The smallest scrap of no news made me cry. People sent sympathy cards, so the mail made me cry. Then my head would hurt again. Then I would sleep some more.

Great-great-aunt Florentine had a quiet, family-only graveside service on Monday, with Preacher Powell saying prayers. I couldn't go—and I cried about that, too—but Daddy told me all about it. Peach didn't go, either. He had taken to bed with a bad cold the day I did, so he had missed out on looking for Dismay as well. He made LOST DOG posters in bed. Mama and Aunt Goldie showed them to me. I could see where Merry had helped him color. I could see where Peach's nose had drip-drip-dripped onto the posters while he had worked.

I hadn't seen Peach for three days, although now and then I'd heard him. Sometimes he'd give off a shriek and wake me out of my sleep, but there was no wailing.

Aunt Goldie visited me. "I called Tucker Elementary School and told them that Peach would be taking an extra week off while he recovered," she said. "Do you know, I think I heard cheering in the background! There must have been a party going on." I smiled at Aunt Goldie with my eyes closed. She said, "You're going to need more than a week off, I'll wager. You take it, Comfort. Sleep now." I did.

I hadn't seen Dismay, either, of course. Each morning I would wake up and expect to feel his shaggy presence at the end of my bed, or his big tongue licking my face—*Comfort! Get up! Come play!*—his collar jangling as I scratched his back and he squirmed with pleasure.

"You said they always come home," I said to Mama each night when she tucked me in and kissed me.

"They always come home," she said, "one way or another. It's not up to us to decide how that homecoming happens."

"What does that mean?" I felt shaky hearing those words.

"It means that no one and nothing is ever gone from us, Comfort."

I didn't get it. "Dismay is gone!" I cried into my pillow. "I need to look for him myself!"

"As soon as you've got your strength back," said Mama, "you can look."

On the fourth day after the flood—another Wednesday—my fever broke and I was well enough to come to the dinner table. Mama walked with me from my bedroom to the kitchen. She smelled like fresh gardenias. Every step I took felt new, like I was learning to walk all over again. So I took each step carefully. Being very sick takes everything out of a person.

Good smells came from the kitchen, and I realized I was hungry finally. The hungry feeling made my steps stronger. The grandfather clock struck noon, and the whistle at the Snapfinger Volunteer Fire Department finished its blowing as I sat down at the table with my family.

Aunt Goldie set an enormous glass of cold milk by my plate. "It's Comfort Snowberger!" she said with mock surprise and real affection in her voice. She kissed me.

"I know!" said Peach, smiling at me from his seat next to Aunt Goldie. He grinned like a possum and sneezed into his napkin.

“Hey,” I said as Daddy pulled my chair out for me and I sat down.

“Fumfort!” said Merry, clapping her hands.

I smiled at her.

Mama had brushed my hair and had put one of Aunt Florentine’s pretty hair combs in it. I liked how it looked. I wore new pajamas Aunt Goldie had bought me. They had suns all over them. I instinctively reached my foot out to caress Dismay under the table, but he wasn’t there. I swallowed hard and tried not to cry. Merry banged her spoon on her high chair and Tidings passed the peas.

“Grace?” said Mama.

“I’ll offer it,” said Aunt Goldie. We held hands while she said, “I would personally like to offer up thanks to every living body in Aurora County, Mississippi, for having the good sense not to die in the past four days.”

“Amen,” said Daddy, who had an empty workroom downstairs.

“We have had enough of death and near death in the Snowberger family!” said Aunt Goldie.

“That’s affirmative,” said Tidings. “Over and out.”

I looked at my family. I felt like I had been gone for a very long time. There was Mama, with her lipstick just right, smiling at Daddy, who was helping my plate with peas. There was Aunt Goldie, flapping out Peach's napkin into his lap, and Peach taking it from her and saying, "I can do it myself." Tidings was already finishing his first helping of meat loaf. My eyes filled with tears. I loved every person sitting at that table. My family. Every one of them. Even Peach. Peach, who would not let Dismay go. Peach, who would have sacrificed himself for my dog. Peach, who had been so brave—braver than I would ever be.

He was blowing on his meat loaf to cool it. His lips flapped as he blew and his face turned a beet red.

"You're gonna blow it right off the fork, Peach," I said.

"Oh." Peach put his fork on his plate. "I'll just wait for it to get cooler." He looked at me. "Thank you, Comfort."

"You're welcome." Peach stared at his meat loaf as if he were watching a special cooling process take place. I said to him, "I never showed you my bottle cap collection."

I could feel everyone's eyes on me.

"No, you didn't," Peach said, staring at me.

"Would you like to see it after dinner?"

"Yes, I would." Peach took a bite of mashed potatoes instead of meat loaf, chewed thoughtfully, and then swallowed. "Am I invited to come to your room to see it?"

"Yes," I said. Just *yes.* Nothing else.

Dinner was good, every bite of it I could eat. Chewing tired me out. I went back to my bedroom. Peach followed me and waited by the door.

I got my bottle cap collection from my closet (I keep it in a big boot box, and it is heavy), climbed into bed, and slipped my feet under the cool covers. Peach clasped his hands together and watched me.

"Okay." I sighed. "Come in."

And he did.

Mama was soon behind him. "You two all right?" she asked.

I nodded my head.

"I'll check on you later, then," she said. She closed the door behind her, and there we were, me and Peach, together and alone again in the middle of an afternoon. I waited for Dismay to trot down the hallway and find us, curious about what we were up to, but of course he didn't. I took the top off my box and motioned to Peach, who came to my bed and looked at Uncle Edisto's life in soda pop.

"Glory, hallelujah!" he whispered.

"I added the RC Colas," I said.

"Can I . . . ? Can I . . . ?"

"Yes," I said.

Peach tried to lift the big box to the floor, but it was so heavy, I was afraid he'd spill it.

"Come up on the bed," I said. "You can sit at the bottom."

He did.

Moon-Glo, Bubble Up, Yoo-Hoo, Whistle, Lemmy Lemonade. The metal caps clinked against one another as Peach sifted them through his fingers. I wondered how he would sort them.

"I miss Uncle Edisto," said Peach.

"So do I."

"He sure liked soda pop," said Peach.

"Aunt Florentine said it would rot his teeth," I said.

"Yeah," said Peach. "But it didn't." He looked at me. "I miss Aunt Florentine, too."

"Me, too."

"Will you still will me these bottle caps, Comfort?" asked Peach.

"I said I would." I wasn't so sure anymore, now that we weren't shivering on a wet rock together, alone and afraid.

"I'm ready to take good care of them," said Peach. He was teary.

"I'm not dead yet!" I said. "Sometimes you are so irritating!"

Tears spilled onto Peach's cheeks. "Dismay is!" he said.

My good dinner turned over in my stomach. "No, he isn't!"

Peach looked at me with shining eyes. "I'm sorry, Comfort! I let him go!"

"It was Declaration's fault," I said quickly. "She scared you, Peach—she sent you down into the oak grove—can't you see that?"

Peach shook his head.

"If we hadn't been down in the grove, it wouldn't have happened!"

Peach couldn't hear me. "Dismay is . . . dead." He shuddered.

"I can't hear this," I told Peach sternly. "Dismay is missing, Peach. *Missing.* And it's not your fault."

Peach pulled a Snowberger's handkerchief out of his pocket. "Are you sure?" he asked. He mopped at his face.

"I'm sure," I said. "I'm completely sure. I know it."

Peach nodded his big head on his scrawny neck and blew his nose, a long honking blow.

"Peach," I said, "can we do this later? I'm real tired. I need to take a nap."

"Oh, sure, Comfort." Peach slid off the bed and looked at me. "I hope you feel better. And . . ."

I waved him away. "I *am* better, Peach. I just need a nap. A long nap."

Peach left the room, and I went to my closet, where I did my best thinking. I hugged Aunt Florentine's pillows to my chest and drank in their lavender smell. Oh, how I longed for everything I had lost! My eyes filled with tears and my head hurt, but I was better. And no one knew Dismay as well as I did. No one knew how to look for him like I did. He would come to me. I would go find my dog.

September 9

Dear Comfort,

You won't answer the phone when I call, and you won't come to the door when I come over.

I have something for you, something important.

I want to bring it over.

Please tell me it is okay to come see you.

Your friend who misses you,
Declaration

September 9
Written from my
almost deathbed,
but I am recovering
(no thanks to you)

<u>Not</u> Dear Declaration,

Don't come near my house or me.

<u>Not</u> your friend, not ever again,

Comfort

CHAPTER 26

The oak grove was once again lush—green, buggy, and hot. Dinner had fortified me, but the bike ride to County Road 2435 tired me out. I considered the bumpy ride down Purgatory Hill and into the grove, where I would lean my bike against an old oak and go find my dog. Rest first, I told myself.

The cemetery called me. It was right there, waiting for me to come lie on soft green grass under a dogwood tree, in the shade. I walked my bike up the little rise and over to Aunt Florentine's grave. We'd rest awhile together. A granite bench had been placed near Uncle Edisto's grave, but I wanted to get closer than a bench would take me.

Great-great-aunt Florentine's grave was mounded with fresh dirt and flower arrangements from the funeral. Great-uncle Edisto rested next to Aunt Florentine. His grave had green grass over it already. The two graves looked cozy, side by side. I sat between them on Uncle Edisto's grass and read the headstones. How beautiful they were!

I had visited Uncle Edisto many times in the six months since he had died. A hand was carved into his granite headstone. A finger pointed upward, toward the blue sky. The inscription under the hand read: *God's finger touched him and he slept.* I loved that.

"I'm willing your bottle cap collection to Peach," I said out loud. Uncle Edisto didn't reply, so I figured that meant the idea was all right. I felt better about it.

Aunt Florentine's headstone would have her death date added to it. Then it would be complete. It had a granite telephone engraved in it. The inscription read: *Jesus called her home.* It was perfect for Aunt Florentine. The only thing better would have been a pair of binoculars with, maybe, *Jesus saw that she was ready.* Because she was.

Old Johnny Mercer would soon take all the wilting flowers away, but he would leave the lavender. Lavender sprayed from two big urns on either side of Aunt Florentine's headstone. It was tied in bunches, in bouquets, in . . . in . . . I looked hard at the urn farthest from me. In it there was a lavender collar—a dog's collar.

I scrambled to my feet and was immediately on my knees in front of the urn. There, in the middle of purple blossoms, was my dog's collar. Dismay! I snatched it and shot to my feet. "Dismay!" I hollered. "Dismay!" I looked all around me, turning and calling for my dog.

Instead I saw Mama. She was walking across the "Bread of Heaven" section of the cemetery, toward me, wearing her apron with a thousand pockets.

"Mama!" I shouted. "Look! It's Dismay's collar! It's still full of lavender the way you fixed it the day of Aunt Florentine's funeral! Look!"

Mama reached for me and hugged me.

I hugged her back, then quickly disentangled myself. I shook Dismay's collar in front of Mama's face. "He got away, Mama! He got out of the oak grove and out of the water! He came looking for us!"

"Where did you find that?" Mama asked.

"It was in the lavender!" I crowed. "Aunt Florentine was holding on to it for me to find! And now we just have to find Dismay—he's got to be here somewhere!" I was out of breath.

"Maybe he is, honey." Mama smoothed my hair away from my face with her hand. "And maybe he isn't."

"What?" My heartbeat pounded in my ears.

"Comfort," she said.

"What is it?" My insides felt like they were going to burst. I clutched Dismay's collar in both hands and held it close to my chest.

Mama had tears in her eyes. "Sit," she said. We sat on the granite bench, although I didn't want to sit down and Mama knew it. She took a breath, touched her tongue to her top lip, then said, "I think there is always hope, Comfort, always hope. But I also believe Dismay is . . . gone."

"Gone where?" I glanced at Aunt Florentine's grave.

"Dead," Mama said simply.

The word suffocated me. "No," I said simply, in return.

"Yes," said Mama. "I think so. You know that we Snowbergers don't mess around about death . . . We try to see it for what it really is . . ."

I tried to take a breath. My words came out tiny, in a small squeak. I held the collar toward Mama, to show her. "His collar . . ."

"I'm sure Tidings put it there," said Mama in an even voice.

"Where did he find it?" I couldn't bear to hear the answer. I pulled my shoulders up around my ears.

"He didn't find it," said Mama. "Declaration did."

A tingling sensation zinged across my shoulders and up my neck. "Declaration?"

"She found it. She was looking for Dismay with her daddy, and she found the collar near . . ." Mama's voice faltered just a little, then she gathered it together again. "In a drainage ditch near Lake Tallyhoma."

"A ditch?" *A ditch? What is a* ditch*?* I couldn't think!

"Comfort, the ditch feeds into the lake."

No! "Please, Mama . . ."

"Sweetheart . . ." Mama's no-nonsense voice was so tender, it made me cry, but I would not let her touch me. I kept Dismay's collar at my chest so Mama couldn't put her arms around me.

"Are you sure?" I whispered.

"Completely sure," answered Mama, looking deep into my eyes.

I looked away. "I can't think like that," I said in that same tiny voice. I shook my head and looked at Dismay's collar.

"Yes, you can," said Mama. She was inches away from me. "We've searched every bit of the grove, of Snapfinger, of the surrounding area—Dismay is gone, Comfort. You will look for him, too, because you'll need to. That will be good. You'll always look for Dismay, in some way. But that water was high and full of debris, full of danger, and Dismay was strong but not strong enough . . . He was swept away in that flood, Comfort. Away from us. Gone."

I thought of Dismay's eyes looking at me, asking me for help. I saw Peach holding on and going under the water. I saw myself prying Peach's fingers away from Dismay's collar. My heart cracked open. I pulled Dismay's collar close to my belly and held myself as I sobbed. "You said he'd come home! You said they always come home!"

"And they do," Mama said. "Those we love live in our hearts forever! We always have them"—she touched my heart—"right here. Always."

"That's not good enough!" I said. "That's nothing!"

"That . . . is everything," said Mama.

"No, it's not!" I said. "Dismay can't be gone; he can't—if he's gone, that means . . . that means I killed him!" Mama pulled me to her and I sobbed into her shoulder. "Mama, I killed him!"

"Sshhhh," said Mama, her hand on the back of my head. "You did no such thing."

"I did! You don't know!"

"*Sshhhh.* You didn't kill your dog, Comfort."

I pushed myself away from her and wiped at my eyes. "I did, Mama. I let him go! I let him go—not Peach. Peach doesn't remember. He almost drowned trying to hold on to Dismay—he would never have let him go! But I did. I told Peach to let go; I told him to!"

Mama held my face in her hands. "Is that what's eating at your heart?"

I nodded my head and sobbed. "I pried his fingers off Dismay's collar when we were in the water. *I* did it. *I* did it!"

"Comfort, it's a miracle you and Peach survived at all in that water—a miracle!"

I put my hands over my face, Dismay's collar pressing into my nose. I could still smell his scent in the collar.

Mama pulled at my hands, but I wouldn't let her have them, so she just held them, against my face. "Comfort—you saved your cousin's life. You did the absolute best thing you could have done, honey. The right thing. What if Peach had drowned? What if you had drowned?"

"Dismay drowned!" I said. Mama pulled me to her and I wailed. "And Peach is *horrible,* with his *stupid* fears and his *stupid* voice and his *stupid* 'Comfort! I've come to *see* you!' Oh, Mama! I don't *want* Peach!"

"I know!" she said, hugging me.

There was a tiny silence and then . . . I started to laugh. What I had said was so true and so ridiculous at the same time. I laughed right through my tears. Mama did, too.

"He ruins everything!" I said, crying again and sitting up to catch my breath.

"I know," Mama said. "He's a mess."

I nodded.

"And you saved him. You chose him over your dog, who you adore."

I nodded.

"Do you know what you did?" Mama asked.

I looked at her through my tears and tried to pay attention.

"You served," said Mama quietly. "You did what needed to be done. That's what it means, Comfort. You did the right thing even when, somewhere deep inside you, you didn't want to. Because you knew, somewhere even deeper, that it was the right thing to do. And . . . by doing the right thing, you saved yourself as well. If you had grabbed on to Dismay, you would have been washed into the floodwater with him! You would be gone now, too!" Mama's face looked stricken. "I don't think I could have survived that." She squared her shoulders. "And who would have helped Peach? You have good instincts, Comfort Snowberger." Then Mama smiled a real smile at me. "I am so proud to know you."

I shuddered, sniffed, and wiped at my nose. Mama dabbed at my face with a Snowberger's handkerchief. "Uncle Edisto always said, 'It takes courage to look life in the eye and say yes to—' What did he call it?"

" 'The messy glory,' " I said.

"Yes, that's it."

"I need to *do* something! I need to do something for Dismay."

Mama kissed the top of my head. My hair stuck out all over the place, but Mama didn't try to smooth it down.

"You and Peach will figure out what to do," said Mama. "You might ask Tidings as well. He misses Dismay, too. He hasn't mowed the grass all week. He just sits on the mower and thinks."

I sniffed a great sniff, and Mama said, "Do you want to tell me what happened between you and Declaration?"

I shook my head. "Not yet."

"She brought the collar to the house last night," said Mama.

"She did?"

Mama nodded. "Since you won't see her, she gave it to Tidings."

"She did?" I wiped at my eyes.

"Why did Tidings put Dismay's collar here, on Aunt Florentine's flowers?" I sniffed another long sniff.

"He said that recovering soldiers should not be disturbed by evidence they aren't ready to assimilate." Mama smiled, but I didn't. "He was upset, too. So he came to the cemetery. Probably he thought it was best to leave the collar with Aunt Florentine until you were better. Dismay is in good company here, don't you think?"

I looked around me at the community of dead people that Uncle Allagash, Uncle Edisto, and then Daddy had buried for so many years. The headstones formed a family. I loved their solid, sturdy feel. I pictured Tidings leaving Dismay's collar in such a soothing place, a place where Dismay might have chosen to come, if he'd been able. I sent a *Thank you!* thought to Tidings, who was a good brother. I would tell him so.

Special to

THE AURORA COUNTY NEWS

THE LIFE AND TIMES OF DISMAY SNOWBERGER

A Life Notice by ***Comfort Snowberger:***
Explorer, Recipe Tester, and Life Reporter

Dismay Snowberger, Funeral Dog Extraordinaire, has departed Our Fair Town for a new home, after giving hope and love to hundreds of folks all over Aurora County during all the years he kept vigil at family funerals.

Here are the facts: Dismay came to Snowberger's seven years ago on this reporter's third birthday. Right in the middle of the ice cream and cake, there was a scratching and a barking at the downstairs kitchen door. When Tidings Snowberger (aged 7 at the time) opened the door, a shaggy black bundle ran inside with his eyes bright and his tail wagging, as if to say (this is an opinion), *I'm hoooome!* It was

Dismay. He danced inside, with his eyes bright and shiny and his tail wagging, so happy to see us.

Edisto Snowberger, wise in All Things Mysterious, said, "He's a gift to us! Let's keep him. He will comfort us in our dismay."

"Our Dismay," said Florentine Snowberger, wise in All Things Lavender. "Come here, Dismay." She tied a piece of string around Dismay's neck and wove some long stems of lavender around and through it.

Dismay Snowberger was dirty and hungry. Tidings Snowberger, wise in All Things Edible and Organizable, gave Dismay a piece of Phoebe Tolbert's Lane cake, which he enjoyed thoroughly. Comfort Snowberger, wise in Putting Two and Two Together, said, "Dismay is my birthday present!" And Joy Snowberger, wise in All Things Family, sighed and said, "Yes, I believe he is."

Bunch Snowberger, wise in Most Things Funereal, said, "We cannot have a dog at funerals and we've nowhere to put him this afternoon."

But Dismay Snowberger, wise in All Ways of the Heart, made himself useful. Dismay Snowberger knew how to serve. He knew what to do at a funeral—attend to the living, honor the dead. And that is what he did, always silent, always reverent, always present. He was a noble dog.

Life will not be the same with Dismay Snowberger gone to a new home. This reporter likes to think of him trotting to the back door of another funeral home (this is a hope, not an opinion) and going to work again, doing what he does best: loving everyone and everything.

There will be a Life Service for Dismay Snowberger at noon on Saturday, Sept. 12, at Snowberger's (of course). Bring a covered dish (and the recipe) and your memories. Although I did not mention Life Services in my article "Top Ten Tips for First-rate Funeral Behavior," the same rules apply. Please, everyone (you know who you are), behave.

Friday morning,
September 11

Dear Comfort,

I read Dismay's Life Notice in the paper. Daddy is bringing you copies this morning, so I am sending this note over with him before I go off to school. You finally made the paper. I am sorry that it happened with such sad news.

Daddy says the whole county will likely show up for Dismay's Life Service.

I wish you would talk to me when I call. I want to come to Dismay's Life Service. Grandmother Lucy says that decorum dictates I stay home unless you tell me it is all right to come. Please say that it is all right with you that I come.

Grandmother Lucy also said that dogs don't have memorial services. I told her that this one does.

Your sad friend,
Declaration

September 11
Written from my closet,
where I do my best thinking

Declaration,
Do not come.

Comfort

Chapter 27

Aunt Goldie and Peach helped me in the kitchen on Friday. Peach dusted the cake pans and looked like a walking bag of flour. Aunt Goldie hummed. Mama worked on flowers, and Daddy helped Tidings mow grass and wash the windows of the Serenity Suite. Snowberger's was spick-and-span, shining in the warm September sun like a beacon in the Snapfinger countryside, calling one, calling all to gather together.

On Saturday I got up before dawn, sat in my closet, and wrote some remarks to give at Dismay's Life Service. I wrote ten pages. Then I stood on my cabbage-roses carpet in my new funeral dress, in my bare feet, surrounded by my things. I missed spending time with my maps, my magazines, my notebooks, my recipes, my world. I missed my dog sitting in the closet with me, dripping his drippy mouth onto my toes. I licked my lips and slipped my feet into my new Sunday school shoes. I rubbed them with a cold biscuit until they squeaked and I could see my reflection in them. I brushed my hair until it shined. I tucked my remarks into the pocket of my new dress along with a freshly folded Snowberger's handkerchief.

"Time to go," I said as I gazed at myself in the mirror. I inhaled deeply and smelled Aunt Florentine's pillows, which had given me so much comfort. I walked across the hallway to Great-great-aunt Florentine's room.

Peach sat at the window seat, staring at the arriving crowd. He looked at me, then back at the crowd. The front parking lot was full to bursting. Folks were parking on the grass, and Tidings was beside himself, running to their car windows, flailing his arms and trying to direct them to the back lot. I giggled at the sight. Peach didn't. His face had a tragic look to it, that old man look.

So I talked to him. "Did you know that Mr. Lawrence Hobgood brought dog biscuits as his covered dish?" Mrs. Elling had brought her chicken-and-potato-chip casserole again, and Kittie Margolis had brought her famous sweet potato–pineapple-grits soufflé in the shape of a dog's head.

"Your mama has buckets of sunflowers downstairs," said Peach in a shaky voice. "They were Dismay's favorite." They were.

"Are you all right?"

Peach shook his head back and forth, back and forth. "I can't go down there," he whispered. He kept his gaze on the arriving cars below us.

"Why not?" Then I added quickly, "You don't have to go."

"I want to go," Peach said. "But I can't." He dripped tears onto Great-great-aunt Florentine's binoculars. "Mama says it is my choice. I'll stay here in Aunt Florentine's room. She always made me feel better." Peach licked his lips. "I just feel so bad."

My heart cramped. "Wait here." I went back to my closet, scooped up one of Great-great-aunt Florentine's lavender pillows, and took it back across the hall before I could think about it too much. "Here," I said to Peach, holding the pillow in front of me. "Remember this?"

"Oh!" said Peach, his face smiling and his eyes shining with tears. "Oh! Oh! Oh!"

"Yeah," I said, smiling back.

"Did Aunt Florentine will her pillows to you?"

"Sort of," I said. "But I feel sure she would have wanted you to have one. So . . . here." I handed Peach the pillow and he clutched it to his chest. " 'Do this in remembrance of me.' That's what Aunt Florentine would say."

"Yes." Peach buried his face in the lavender pillow and said, in a muffled voice, "I'm so sorry, Comfort. This is all my fault."

My heart couldn't stand it another minute. Uncle Edisto's searchlight of truth was shining on me. "It wasn't your fault, Peach." And while Peach kept his face in the pillow, I told him, "You didn't let Dismay go. I did. I uncurled your fingers and I told you to let him go."

Peach lifted his face. "You did?"

I nodded. "You didn't even hear me. You were almost underwater yourself. You would never have let Dismay go."

"Are you sure?" Peach whispered. "You're not making it up?"

"I wouldn't make this up. I told you to let him go. I did it." I felt tears rising in the back of my throat. I willed them to wait, but they wouldn't. They spilled all over me, and I cried, right in front of Peach. I sat on the cedar chest at the end of Aunt Florentine's bed and tried to stop crying, but my tears kept coming, salty and fat and full of feeling.

When I glanced at Peach, the ancient lines and wrinkles on his face had smoothed out. Tears slipped down his pale cheeks.

I stood and turned to go. "I'll meet you downstairs if you decide to come."

"Comfort?"

"What?"

Peach put his pillow on the end of Aunt Florentine's bed, took a deep breath, and said, "I will be there with bells on."

from:

Fantastic (and Fun) Funeral Food for Family and Friends

By Comfort and Florentine Snowberger

Mrs. Elling's Chicken and Potato Chip Casserole

Preheat the oven to 400 degrees.

Here are the ingredients (more or less):

Cooked chicken (just cut up leftover chicken from a previous meal)

Leftover rice, enough to fill your cereal bowl (two cups if you're Tidings)

One can of condensed cream-of-chicken (or cream-of-mushroom, or any other cream of your choice) soup

One enormous spoonful of mayonnaise (not a dollop; a glob)

Chopped-up onions and celery—you be the judge of how much (You can leave onions and celery out of this recipe, but we're not responsible for taste or lack of compliments)

At least one can of mandarin oranges, drained well
Salt and pepper to taste
A hunk of your favorite cheese, grated (don't skimp here)
A whole bag of Mrs. B's Southern Style Potato Chips, crushed (poke a hole in it with a fork and bang on the bag with a rolling pin before you open it)

Directions:
In a big (we do mean big) bowl, combine all these ingredients except the cheese and potato chips. Spread this mixture into a 9x13 baking pan (or use a molded cake pan for decorative effect on special occasions). On top of the mixture, sprinkle your grated cheese. On top of the cheese put your crushed potato chips—don't be stingy with the potato chips. Bake this comforting casserole in the preheated oven for about 20 minutes, or until the potato chips are lightly browned.

Feeds multitudes and brings on sincere compliments.

Chapter 28

I took the back stairs by myself. A torrent of people greeted me as I neared the Serenity Suite. They said they were so glad to see me. They told me how brave I had been. They complimented me on Dismay's Life Notice, and I told them to tell Mr. Johnson.

"I'm honored to be of service," Mr. Johnson said to me when I thanked him. He patted on me like I was Dismay. Declaration hadn't come. *Good.* I didn't mention it to Mr. Johnson, and he didn't say anything to me about it, either.

Mama's flowers were poked into every corner and onto every surface—bachelor's buttons, snapdragons, asters, Shasta daisies, and huge buckets of sunflowers. I almost couldn't look at them.

Peach came down the grand front staircase with Aunt Goldie, keeping his gaze intently on the front doors, as if he might hear Dismay barking outside any moment. He was carrying Aunt Florentine's pillow with him. People made a pathway for Peach, and he actually smiled as he made his way to the Serenity Suite.

Tidings marshaled people to their seats. "We've run out of Snowberger's handkerchiefs!" he murmured to me as I passed him.

"Kleenex," I whispered.

"We're out of that, too. The troops are fortifying themselves!"

"We can't think of everything."

Mama came in with a basket of freshly ironed and folded handkerchiefs and put them on the table by the door. "Bless Lurleen's heart," she said, smiling at me. "She knew we'd need extras today."

Daddy was right behind Mama, carrying Merry, who was singing, to the tune of "Jingle Bells": "Handkerchief, sniff-sniff-sniff. Blow-blow-blow away!"

"Can you tell she's been ironing with Lurleen?" Daddy asked. He patted my shoulder. "How you doing, honey?"

"I'm fine." My stomach was full of bumblebees.

Preacher Powell took his place at the front of the Serenity Suite, where, instead of a casket, Tidings and I had put Dismay's bed on the rolling platform along with several pictures of Dismay that Peach had taken with the camera Great-uncle Edisto had willed to him. Dismay's lavender collar stayed upstairs in my room. I didn't want to share it with anybody.

Mrs. Powell started playing "For the Beauty of the Earth," and folks spontaneously began to sing:

> *"For the beauty of the earth*
> *For the glory of the skies,*
> *For the love which from our birth*
> *Over and around us lies!"*

That's when my heart swelled up so fast, it closed my throat and I could hardly breathe. I sat down with a *thunk*.

"You all right, Comfort?" asked Tidings.

I nodded. My face felt hot.

"Fumfort!" said Merry. She was standing at my knees. She hugged them fiercely with her short arms and began showering them with little kisses.

Mama scooped up Merry and sat next to me. She

kissed my head. Peach was on the other side of Mama. He sat calmly, without his face in Aunt Goldie's armpit. Aunt Goldie wore all green, "a remembrance color," she'd said.

Preacher Powell began again, like he'd begun 248 times before.

"Dearly beloved! We are here to celebrate life!"

"Amen!" said Homer Hindman.

"Amen!" said Peach.

Preacher Powell stopped cold. Necks craned and people shuffled in their chairs.

"Peach?" asked Preacher Powell.

"Peach!" Aunt Goldie beamed.

"Peace!" Merry clapped her hands together.

Peach grinned and sat up straighter. I clasped my hands together. My heart was pounding hard in my chest—*Dismay, Dismay, Dismay!*

"Let us celebrate the gift that Dismay Snowberger *is*"—Preacher Powell looked to me for emphasis—"to his family, his community, and the world."

My pulse thrummed in my ears.

Tidings nudged me with his elbow. "Your turn."

I shook my head and stared into my lap.

Preacher Powell kept going. "Ahh . . . As I understand the order of this . . . er . . . most unusual event—

a Life Service!—the family has asked that we all share stories about Dismay Snowberger, funeral dog extraordinaire, and then join them for a meal outside under the pecan trees, where Dismay was fond of sleeping. I hope you brought your lawn chairs!" Preacher Powell chuckled and a few folks murmured back. He cleared his throat. "Ahem. Okay. Who would like to go first with their remembrance?"

Remembrance. The word sounded so final. It was brilliantly sunny outside, but at that moment I felt like I was somewhere else—I heard rain falling all around me. Rain and the roaring wind in the trees, the sound of Peach screaming and Dismay paddling and me yelling *Let him go!* and the sight of Dismay tumbling and swirling away from me. Where did he come to rest? *Oh, what had happened to my dog?* I covered my face with my hands.

Mama put her arm around me and leaned her head toward mine. "Shall we stop?"

I shook my head in my hands. I came back to myself. I listened.

One by one our friends and neighbors stood to talk about Dismay, about how he helped them, how he loved them, how happy he was to see them, how he attended their loved ones, never leaving their sides, always friendly, always respectful, always a happy dog. Their stories comforted me at first, but then they made me miss my dog even more.

"Dismay was—*is*—a feel-good dog!" said Mr. Johnson.

After every memory Peach would say "Amen!" and folks would chuckle. He got very good at it.

Finally, Preacher Powell said to me, "Comfort?"

I lifted my face from my hands.

"Are you ready to say a few words?"

Tidings whispered to me, "You don't have to . . ."

But I wanted to. I fumbled in my pocket for my remarks. There they were. I looked at Peach. His whole face was shining, smiling at me. He was perfect. A perfect Peach. He whispered across Mama to me, "I am here with bells on!" I nodded. I started to stand up, but I couldn't—I tilted. Tidings grabbed me and helped me sit back down. He and Mama exchanged a look. I looked at Preacher Powell for help.

"'All Things Bright and Beautiful'!" said Preacher Powell. "We will sing Edisto Snowberger's version of this hymn, which you will find as song number seventy-two from Snowberger's Funeral Home Book of Suggested Songs for Significant Occasions. It was to be sung at the end of our service, but we'll just move it up to here, because . . . Well, because I say so!" He chuckled louder this time, and more folks laughed with him. He seemed pleased. "Mrs. Powell, would you play?"

Everyone but me stood to the opening of the hymn. As the singing started and I heard the words, I thought of *Dismay, Dismay, Dismay!*—bright and beautiful, great and small, wise and wonderful . . . and lost to me. Lost.

I stared at the tops of my shiny new shoes. I willed myself to stand. And as the singing ended and folks sat down, I stood up. I willed myself to walk to the podium. I pulled my remarks from my pocket and smoothed them out. I lifted my head and stared at our friends who packed the Serenity Suite. I licked my lips and swallowed.

I opened my mouth, but no words came out.

And then, from a seat in the back of the room near the doors to the Serenity Suite, Declaration rose.

CHAPTER 29

I must have looked mighty surprised, because all heads turned toward the back of the room, where Declaration stood with her hands held in front of her. She looked straight at me. I didn't know what to say. I was almost glad to see her.

"I have a memory to share," she said.

I almost said, No one wants to hear your memory, but I wanted to know what it was, so I said, "Go ahead."

Declaration smoothed at her hair under her hat. Her voice had a shaky tone to it. She said, "I met Dismay when I was four and my mother . . . died. We came to Snowberger's. Dismay was bigger than I was. I was scared of him, but Comfort showed me how to pet him and feed him and how to scratch him behind his ears." She stopped. Her face was red. She took a breath and continued. "I'm not much for dogs. But Dismay introduced me to Comfort, my best friend. And he made me laugh that day when everyone was so sad. He helped me not to miss my mama so much that day."

Declaration started to sit but then stood up again and said, "Missing people you love is hard."

She sat down for good. Phoebe Tolbert cried into her Snowberger's handkerchief. Mr. Johnson stood up and began to walk back to Declaration, but next to Declaration sat Grandmother Lucy, who waved a gloved hand toward Mr. Johnson in a *She's-all-right-let-her-be-I'm-right-here-with-her* way. Mr. Johnson nodded and stayed where he was.

So did I. Soon, every eye was on me again.

I looked at my ten pages of remarks. Declaration had said what I wanted to say. Missing people—and dogs—you love is hard. It hurts your heart. That's what I wanted to say. Everyone else had said every good thing about Dismay. They already knew what a good dog he was. So I put my remarks aside and tried to reach into my hurting heart for something to say.

"Fumfort!" said Merry in a too loud whisper.

I lifted some fingers toward her and she waved. I looked at my family—everyone in that room was family—and I said: "I miss my dog."

My throat swelled until it hurt, and tears stung the inside of my nose. I thought of something else, so I said it: "I hope he comes home."

"Amen," said Peach.

"Amen," said Homer Hindman and Phoebe Tolbert and then a chorus of folks.

And then a new thought came to me like a slender stream of hope, filling me with a new understanding. "And," I said, hoping they would understand, hoping Dismay would understand, too: "I am glad to be alive."

"Amen!" said Daddy and Mama together.

"Alive!" said Merry.

"Yes!" said everyone.

And then there was laughing.

Chapter 30

The leaves fell from the trees and the snap of fall was in the air. At Snowberger's the smells of pumpkin pie and corn bread dressing upstairs mingled with the etherlike smells from downstairs, where Daddy worked on Myrtis Rogers, getting her ready for a Saturday funeral. Merry napped and Mama worked in the flower shop, making a Thanksgiving arrangement for our dinner table. Tidings raked around the magnolia trees by the front parking lot—he didn't like leaves bothering his grass. Peach and Aunt Goldie had arrived from Atlanta, and Aunt Goldie was roasting a turkey in the oven in a paper bag—"My secret recipe!" She taught

Peach how to break pecans into bits for the pecan pie, and she finally released me from chopping celery and onions and had me set the table. Then she said Peach and I could go.

"Wear your watch!" she called to Peach. "Be back by two thirty!"

The Thanksgiving Day sunshine was warm on our backs as we walked down County Road 2435, past the stubble that was left from the corn that had been harvested from Homer Hindman's field just the week before. As we stepped off the dirt road and into the oak grove, we looked at each other, but we didn't say a word. We walked down Purgatory Hill together. A thousand songbirds greeted us as we walked beneath the open canopy of trees in the oak grove. We crossed burbling Snapfinger Creek on the little footbridge that Tidings had built.

When we reached the rose of Sharon bushes, Peach stopped, ran his fingers across the graceful branches, and then looked to the top of Listening Rock. "I'm ready," he said.

I listened to our gritty footfalls as we climbed. Peach puffed and stopped to rest three times (so I stopped with him), but he never complained. I waited for him in silence each time, studying the metamorphic marvel we were walking on.

At the top Peach broke into a wide grin. "It's amazing! You can see everything! Just like Uncle Edisto said!" He inched himself on his bottom, like a shy crab, toward the tip-top of the slope, to the highest spot, where he sat, washed in sunlight, surveying the kingdom that was Snowberger's. He blinked in the breeze that tugged at his slicked-down hair. I sat beside him. Old Johnny Mercer had finished digging Myrtis Rogers's grave and had set the green tarp over it. It looked like a peaceful grave.

"There's Uncle Edisto's grave," said Peach, pointing to the Bread of Heaven section of the Snapfinger Cemetery.

"Aunt Florentine's, too." I left it at that.

I visited Uncle Edisto and Aunt Florentine in the cemetery quite a bit. I enjoyed eating a tuner-fish sandwich and catching them up on the news. I read Aunt Florentine my funeral write-ups. We talked geography.

"No grave for Dismay," said Peach.

"No."

"I still wait for him to come home," said Peach.

"Me, too."

"You never know, Comfort," said Peach. "You just never ever know what the next good or bad thing will be."

"That's for sure."

"Life just keeps changing, all the time, every minute!"

"Be quiet, Peach. I can't think."

The breeze fanned my face while I took stock. One: I still woke up in the morning listening for Dismay's *tap-tap-tap*ping down the hallway, coming to get me up. That hadn't changed. It wasn't a good thing. Two: I still wore my Snowberger's baseball cap and my lime green shorts, and I still sat in my closet, where I did my homework and made my plans. That hadn't changed. That was a good thing. Three: Life *was* full of surprises, and not all of them were good. But some were.

Listening Rock baked in the sun while geese flew overhead, honking. Because the leaves were off the trees, I could hear Snapfinger Creek bubbling over the rocks.

"I like it up here," said Peach. "It's calming."

"Yes it is."

The sound of gritty footfalls came, and I turned to see Declaration making the last climbing steps up Listening Rock. She was wearing her Sunday school dress and hat and gloves. She was breathing hard, catching her breath. She kept her eyes on me. My heart began a little *thump-thump* in my chest. Declaration and I hardly talked anymore. Everything had been too complicated between us.

"Hey," Declaration said.

"Hey," I said back.

"Did you know Daddy and I were invited for Thanksgiving dinner?"

"I know." I had told Mama I didn't have anything to talk to Declaration about. Mama had said I'd figure it out.

Declaration looked at Peach. "Hey, Peach."

Peach raised a hand but said nothing.

"Well . . . ," said Declaration.

I didn't help her.

She fidgeted. "Can I sit down?"

I shrugged. I wanted her to. I didn't.

Declaration stepped gingerly, carefully, toward us—toward the highest point of Listening Rock, where she sat down next to me, which put me in the middle between her and Peach. The three of us sat there for a long time, silent, beneath the ever-changing clouds, surrounded by a dancing breeze. We stared out at

Snapfinger Cemetery, and the blacktopped Rural Route 2 that stretched out to bigger roads across all of Mississippi and beyond. We sat under a wide autumn sky, a sky that sheltered us all, even my Dismay. Big, black, shaggy Dismay, with his shiny dog eyes—*Is everything all right?*—and his wagging dog tail—*I'm just so glad to be here!*—and his goofy dog grin, so willing to love everybody.

Peach looked at his watch. "It's time to go."

"How are you, Peach?" said Declaration, looking across me to my cousin.

"I might be moving," said Peach, looking back.

"You might?"

"Mama and me might move to Snapfinger when school lets out next summer. We would live at Snowberger's."

"Is that so?" said Declaration as the three of us made our way down Listening Rock.

Now, Peach didn't know if he was moving or not. He'd been sitting across from me in the kitchen that morning, eating Chocolate Buzz Krispies and listening to Mama and Aunt Goldie talk about possibilities. We had exchanged a look over the zinnias. Snowberger's was so much emptier than it had ever been. It echoed with the voices of Great-uncle Edisto, Great-great-aunt Florentine, and Dismay. It wasn't the same place for me, or for Peach, I could tell.

"Well, good for you, Peach," said Declaration.

"Yeah," said Peach, dodging a scrub pine and picking his way carefully on the rock. We walked in silence to the bottom and soon found ourselves once again on County Road 2435 together.

"Maybe I can come visit sometime after you move," said Declaration. "I'm a good marbles player. I've got a shooter that's a butterfly agate."

"Really!" exclaimed Peach. He picked up his step. The orange-pebbled road crunched smartly under his hard-soled shoes. "Wow!"

"When did you learn to play marbles?" I asked Declaration.

"My grandmother Lucy taught me," said Declaration. "She collected marbles when she was young, and she has willed her entire collection to me."

"They must be ancient," I said.

"Possibly Egyptian," said Declaration.

She almost smiled at me. I almost smiled back.

"Marbles!" Peach was almost exploding with enthusiasm. "This is so exciting!" He skipped ahead of us and turned back to face me.

I almost ran into him. "Stop it, Peach!" I said, feeling

pretty explosive myself. "Stop being so . . . Peach-like! Sometimes you irritate the hound out of me!"

"What possibilities!" he crowed, as if he hadn't even heard me. "What joy! Maybe we can play today, Declaration!"

"That would be fine," said Declaration.

Good, I thought. *Fine.* Let Declaration play marbles with Peach. Let them become fast friends! I walked right past them.

"Commmforrrt! Don't go! Waaaaaiit!" Peach began a familiar whine.

I whirled around so I could order him to stop, but he had stopped himself. So I stopped, too. I stared into my cousin's shining eyes. Then I looked into Declaration's eyes. And I saw in their faces what had been in Dismay's eyes in that last moment I'd seen him—grief and fear and hope and love somehow woven together, somehow connected. All the messy glory.

Peach quivered with his overwrought feelings, trying to pull himself together. I pulled myself together, too. My heart began a *what's-next, what's-next, what's-next* beat.

The afternoon was alive with the racket of a thousand different songbirds calling to us from the grove, surrounding us with their chants, their hymns, their lullabies.

"Comfort," Peach whispered. "It's *Thanksgiving,* and I've come to *see* you!"

I glanced toward the cemetery, then toward home. I swallowed hard and took a breath. And, as I did, my heart melted around the sweetness and sadness of the world and I responded to my cousin . . . to life.

"Okay," I said. "Come *see* me then."